BOARDWALK BREEZES

MAGNOLIA KEY
BOOK SEVEN

KAY CORRELL

ZURA LU PUBLISHING LLC

Published by Zura Lu Publishing LLC

ABOUT THIS BOOK

On Magnolia Key, everyone knows your name—and your past

Beverly Mooney has spent decades building a quiet life on Magnolia Key, where the scent of sea air mingles with fresh-brewed coffee and the boardwalk holds memories too bittersweet to revisit. But then Cliff Griffin—her high school heartbreak turned ambitious developer—returns with plans for a towering high-rise that could change everything.

Some see opportunity. Others see the loss of the town's charm. Beverly sees the man who broke her heart long ago stepping back into her world with too much confidence and far too many memories.

As neighbors take sides and old tensions rise, Beverly finds herself torn between preserving the past and navigating an uncertain future. Then a hurricane shifts course, forcing everyone to face what truly matters.

Boardwalk Breezes is a story of second chances, stubborn hearts, and the fight to protect what matters most.

*This book is dedicated to those people in our life who
somehow become our best friends.
The person we can call in the middle of the night if we need
them. The person who knows all our secrets. Who has shared
our joys and our deepest sorrows.
May you always have a best friend to share your journey.*

between series - with Josephine and Paul from The Letter.)

LIGHTHOUSE POINT ~ THE SERIES
Wish Upon a Shell - Book One
Wedding on the Beach - Book Two
Love at the Lighthouse - Book Three
Cottage near the Point - Book Four
Return to the Island - Book Five
Bungalow by the Bay - Book Six
Christmas Comes to Lighthouse Point - Book Seven

CHARMING INN ~ Return to Lighthouse Point
One Simple Wish - Book One
Two of a Kind - Book Two
Three Little Things - Book Three
Four Short Weeks - Book Four
Five Years or So - Book Five
Six Hours Away - Book Six
Charming Christmas - Book Seven

SWEET RIVER ~ THE SERIES
A Dream to Believe in - Book One
A Memory to Cherish - Book Two
A Song to Remember - Book Three
A Time to Forgive - Book Four
A Summer of Secrets - Book Five
A Moment in the Moonlight - Book Six

MOONBEAM BAY ~ THE SERIES

The Parker Women - Book One
The Parker Cafe - Book Two
A Heather Parker Original - Book Three
The Parker Family Secret - Book Four
Grace Parker's Peach Pie - Book Five
The Perks of Being a Parker - Book Six

BLUE HERON COTTAGES ~ THE SERIES

Memories of the Beach - Book One
Walks along the Shore - Book Two
Bookshop near the Coast - Book Three
Restaurant on the Wharf - Book Four
Lilacs by the Sea - Book Five
Flower Shop on Magnolia - Book Six
Christmas by the Bay - Book Seven
Sea Glass from the Past - Book Eight

MAGNOLIA KEY ~ THE SERIES

Saltwater Sunrise - Book One
Encore Echoes - Book Two
Coastal Candlelight - Book Three
Tidal Treasures - Book Four
Bayside Beginnings - Book Five
Seaside Sunshine - Book Six
Boardwalk Breezes - Book Seven

CHRISTMAS SEASHELLS AND SNOWFLAKES

Seaside Christmas Wishes

WIND CHIME BEACH ~ A stand-alone novel

INDIGO BAY ~
Sweet Days by the Bay - Kay's Complete Collection
of stories in the Indigo Bay series

Sign up for my newsletter at my website *kaycorrell.com*
to make sure you don't miss any new releases or
sales.

CHAPTER 1

Beverly paused as she wiped down the counter at Coastal Coffee, her movements slower than usual. The day's rush had dwindled, leaving only the lingering scent of coffee and pastries in the air.

"You've been quiet today." Maxine settled onto one of the barstools, chin propped in her hand.

"Just thinking about the town council meeting tomorrow." She tossed the cleaning rag into a bucket beneath the counter. "Cliff's project to build the high-rise at the end of the boardwalk is all anyone talks about anymore."

"You're right. I heard plenty of our customers talking about it today." Her best friend's eyes narrowed. "But that's not what's really bothering you, is it?"

She let out a long breath and leaned against the

counter. "It's part of it, but not all that's bothering me."

"It's Cliff, isn't it? The fact that it's Cliff who wants to do this?"

"I thought he understood what makes this place special." She motioned toward the window, where the boardwalk stretched toward the water. "Now he wants to change everything."

"People change, Bev."

"Do they? Because from where I'm standing, he's the same selfish boy who left me waiting at the ferry all those years ago without a word."

Maxine reached across the counter and squeezed her hand. "I'm sorry."

"It doesn't matter now." She pulled away, busying herself with organizing the coffee cups. "What matters now is protecting our town from becoming another overdeveloped tourist trap."

"Maybe. But fighting this project means dealing with Cliff, and I'm worried about what that's doing to you."

"I'm fine."

Maxine looked at her skeptically. "You're not fine. You're reliving old hurts whenever his name comes up in conversation. And in this town, his name comes up a lot these days."

"I thought I was over it. Thirty-seven years is a long time to hold onto teenage heartbreak." And why did she know exactly how many years it had been? That annoyed her.

"Some wounds leave deeper scars than others." Maxine got up, walked around the counter, and wrapped her arm around Beverly's shoulders. "Especially when they never really healed in the first place."

She smiled. "Have I told you lately how glad I am that you returned to Magnolia Key? And that you work here at the shop now?"

"I'm glad I moved home, too."

She grabbed two coffee cups. "Let's take a break before we finish up."

"Sounds good to me."

Beverly poured the coffee, and they headed over to a nearby table. She stretched out her legs, glad to be off her feet for a bit. "The council meeting tomorrow is going to be heated. I've heard both sides all day in here."

"I did too." Maxine nodded.

"This morning, I had Tim Marshall in here talking about how his son might be able to get a good job if the development goes through. Right now, most of the young people have to leave the island to find work." She set her cup down. "Then an hour later, Sarah Smith was going on about how a high-rise would destroy the view from her shop."

"Both make good points."

"I know. That's what makes this so difficult."

She glanced out the window at the street where locals and tourists strolled past the shops. "I remember when we were kids and how many of our friends had to move away after high school."

"Like Danny. Remember him? He left town because there wasn't enough work here."

"Exactly." She traced her finger around the rim of her coffee cup. "But then I think about what makes this place special. The way you can see the water from almost anywhere. How everyone knows each other. The peace and quiet."

"A six-story building would change things."

"More than just the building. It would bring more tourists and more traffic. Probably more shops catering to visitors rather than locals." She shook her head. "I heard talk Jerry might have to close his grocery store if it goes through."

"Really? But they've been here forever. Generations of his family have run the store."

"Three generations. But Jerry says if the development happens, a big chain store will want to come in and they won't be able to compete. This morning some construction workers were talking about the jobs it would create. Good-paying jobs. And not just during construction. There would be maintenance positions, security, and cleaning staff."

"The town could use that."

"It could. But at what cost?" She looked around her coffee shop. "Would people still want to come sit here, drink coffee, and chat with their neighbors if we become just another tourist spot? Would they still feel that sense of community? We have regular visitors, families that have been coming to the island for years. Will they want to come here if the whole feeling of the island changes?"

"Some change is inevitable."

"But once it starts, you can't go back. Look at how many quaint Florida towns are now peppered with high-rises."

"The council seems split too, from what I hear." Maxine took a sip of her coffee.

"They are. The mayor is for it. He says we need the tax revenue. But Rachel and George are against it. The others on the council..." She shrugged. "They're waiting to hear what people say at the meeting before deciding."

"Sounds like tomorrow night's meeting will be interesting."

"That's one word for it." She stood and walked to the window. "You know what bothers me most? The way it's dividing people. Usually, when something comes up, we all pull together. But this..." She turned back to Maxine. "I've seen lifelong friends arguing about it. The Petersons and the Grants aren't speaking to each other anymore over it."

"Small towns can be like that. People feel strongly about their home."

"They do. And everyone has valid points on both sides. I just side with keeping with our building code. No high-rises. I like Magnolia Key just like it is." She returned to her seat. "I just wish there was a way to bring new opportunities without losing what makes this place special."

"And what does your heart tell you about all of this?"

"My heart?" She gave a small laugh. "My heart is probably the last thing I should listen to when it comes to anything involving Cliff Griffin."

CHAPTER 2

Cliff eased his Mercedes off the ferry, the familiar sights of the island stretching before him. He couldn't wait for the bridge to be finished to connect the mainland to the island. It would help cut construction costs on his building as well as make it easier for guests to get to the island and fill his hotel.

As he pulled onto Main Street, the late afternoon sun cast long shadows across the storefronts with their faded paint and weather-worn signs exactly as he remembered. His car purred down the street in blunt contrast to the rustic charm surrounding him.

The scent of jasmine drifted through his open window, mixed with salt air. He'd forgotten that particular combination that seemed so uniquely Magnolia Key. The hanging baskets outside the shops swayed in the breeze, spilling over with bright flowers. Some things never changed.

Several people on the sidewalk stopped to stare as he drove past. Mrs. Henderson, his old math teacher, gave a slight head shake before turning away. Jake, who owned the hardware store, offered a friendly wave. The town remained divided on his development plans, just as they'd been divided on everything else he'd ever done.

He pulled into a spot near city hall and cut the engine. The building's white columns and weather vane looked exactly the same as when he'd played on these steps as a kid, back before everything got complicated.

Through the window of the gift shop, he caught Patty Miller's wide-eyed gaze before she ducked behind a display. Two teenagers walking past whispered and pointed, probably having heard all about the troublemaker son coming home to build his high-rise.

He stepped out of his car, straightening his suit jacket. A few unfamiliar faces hurried past, likely some of the new residents who'd moved to the island in recent years. But mostly he saw the same people who'd watched him grow up and who still remembered him as that wild kid.

The sea breeze ruffled his hair as he grabbed his briefcase from the passenger seat. He had every right to be here, to develop his property as he saw fit. If only he could convince the rest of them to see the potential in his plans.

He spotted his mother before she saw him. Eleanor Griffin stood on the sidewalk outside of the drugstore, her cream-colored dress and matching shoes pristine as always. Her silver hair caught the sunlight, styled in the same perfect waves she'd worn for decades. She clutched a clipboard in her hands. No doubt for some fundraising event. She never stopped with her committees and causes.

The urge to duck into the nearest shop hit him hard. But he wasn't that teenage boy anymore, trying to escape her disappointment.

"Cliff." Her voice carried down the street. Several people turned to watch, including old Mrs. Peterson sweeping her shop's front step.

"Mother." He kept his voice pleasant, if not quite friendly. "You're looking well."

"You're stirring up trouble again." The words cracked like a whip. She tapped her perfectly manicured nails against the clipboard. "As if this town needs more upheaval."

He noticed Patty from the gift shop had stepped outside her door, pretending to arrange a display while clearly straining to hear every word.

"Progress isn't trouble, Mother. The development will bring jobs and tourism dollars. The town needs this kind of economic boost." The practiced pitch rolled off his tongue, but his insides twisted at her familiar frown. The one that said he'd disappointed her yet again.

"We don't need that kind of progress. This isn't Miami Beach. Your father would never have supported this scheme."

His chest tightened at the mention of his father, but he kept his easy smile in place. "Times change. Magnolia Key needs to adapt or it'll get left behind. The high-rise will blend with the town's character while bringing in vital revenue."

Though he actually thought his father would approve of this project. The man had always been after the dollars, and this project, if he could make it happen, was sure to bring in lots of profit.

More people gathered on the sidewalk, some not even pretending they weren't listening. His mother's lips pressed into a thin line as she shook her head.

"You've always done exactly what you wanted, haven't you? Never mind what's best for anyone else." The words hit their mark, the same as they had when he was young. His stomach churned with the familiar feeling of failing to measure up.

But he wasn't that kid anymore. He had built a successful business and made something of himself. Even if it never seemed to be enough for her.

"I know what I'm doing, Mother. This project will benefit everyone, including you, if you'd let it."

Her gaze sharpened, her voice lowering. "You may have the council's ear for now, but don't think that guarantees anything. There's mounting opposition, Cliff. Councilman Johnson—you remember George—is rallying support against the project. And Rachel Masters is convinced it'll ruin the island's charm."

He fought the urge to roll his eyes. Of course she would have the pulse of every council member's opinion. Her intimate knowledge of town politics was both impressive and irritating, reminding him why she still remained a force to be reckoned with.

"I'm well aware of the opposition. But I have support too. Times are changing, and this development is the future of Magnolia Key."

"This monstrosity will destroy the very character of our town. The charm, the history. Is that really what you want your legacy to be?"

Anger flashed through him, hot and sharp. "Progress isn't a dirty word, Mother. The island can't stay frozen in time forever. Change is necessary for growth."

"Growth?" she scoffed. "Is that what you call it? Paving over our heritage for a quick buck?"

He took a deep breath, trying to rein in his temper. "It's not just about money. Think of the jobs this project will bring. Construction work, hospitality positions, and new retail spaces. Lots of guests at the hotel. It'll be a boost to the whole economy."

His mother waved a dismissive hand. "A few

low-paying jobs are hardly worth the cost. This town has survived for generations without turning into a tourist trap. We don't need your high-rise to save us."

Frustration simmered through him. She'd never understood his vision, even when he was a kid with big dreams. To her, he'd always be that wild child who couldn't do anything right.

He put on a smile, a gesture of confidence he didn't quite feel. "The town council will decide what's best for Magnolia Key. And I believe they'll see the value in my proposal."

"Oh, they'll decide all right." His mother's tone held a note of warning. "But don't assume you know which way the winds will blow. There are a lot of people who won't take kindly to an outsider trying to change our way of life. Even if that outsider has Griffin blood."

The word outsider stung more than he cared to admit. He'd grown up here, the same as her. But in her eyes, he'd lost the right to call Magnolia Key home the moment he left.

"I'm not an outsider, Mother. And I'm not trying to ruin anything. I'm trying to help this town grow. To give it a future."

"The future of Magnolia Key is not yours to decide." She clutched her clipboard tighter, as if it were a shield against his arguments. "And if you can't see the value in preserving our heritage, then perhaps you never truly understood this town at all."

With that, she turned on her heel and marched down the sidewalk, her head held high. The small crowd that had gathered quickly dispersed, but he could feel their stares boring into his back.

He stood there a moment, watching her retreating form. The sun dipped lower on the horizon, painting the street in shades of gold and shadow. The same street he'd walked a thousand times as a boy, dreaming of a life beyond the island's shores.

But now, standing here in his tailored suit with his expensive car parked behind him, those dreams felt hollow somehow. The past clung to him, chattering about all he'd left behind.

He shook his head, pushing the thoughts away. He couldn't change the past, but he could shape the future. And Magnolia Key's future was bright, whether his mother chose to see it or not.

With a deep breath, he turned toward city hall, his steps purposeful on the sun-warmed pavement. The mayor awaited, and he had a development to fight for. No matter how much opposition he faced, he wouldn't let this town get left behind. Even if it meant becoming the villain in his mother's eyes once again.

CHAPTER 3

As Beverly stepped into the town hall, the familiar faces of her neighbors divided like opposing teams at a football game. On one side sat Rachel Masters, with her group from the historical society. On the other, Tim Marshall and several business owners who supported progress and development. These people usually shared friendly waves and stopped to chat at Coastal Coffee. Now they barely looked at each other.

She scanned the crowd, searching for an empty seat, when her gaze landed on Cliff. Her heart stuttered, and her feet refused to move. He wore a dark suit that fit his broad shoulders perfectly. She hated that he still affected her this way after all these years.

"We should take a seat." Miss Eleanor's voice

broke through her paralysis. The older woman pointed toward some empty chairs near the front.

She followed Miss Eleanor, keeping her eyes ahead to avoid looking at Cliff again. She settled into the wooden chair, smoothing her skirt and pulling out her phone to check the time. The mayor should start soon.

Jonah slipped into the empty chair by Miss Eleanor and smiled at her. "Sorry, Ellie. Running a bit late." He took her hand in his.

It still surprised Beverly just a bit to see Miss Eleanor and Jonah. Miss Eleanor had been a widow for so long and never dated a soul. Then Jonah returned and all that changed. She had her second chance with him.

Beverly turned back to the front as the mayor stepped up to the podium and tapped the microphone. "Good evening, everyone. Tonight's agenda focuses on the proposed development at the end of the boardwalk. Mr. Griffin will present his plans, followed by public comments."

Cliff approached the podium, carrying a portfolio. He opened it and began setting up large mounted boards on easels. The renderings showed gleaming glass and steel rising above the boardwalk, modern and sleek against the backdrop of the ocean.

"Thank you, Mayor." Cliff's voice carried clearly through the room. "The proposed development includes retail space on the ground floor, a floor of conference rooms and hotel dining, and four floors of hotel rooms. Our economic impact study projects over a hundred permanent jobs will be created along with a significant increase in tax revenue for Magnolia Key."

Beverly watched as he moved confidently through his presentation, gesturing to charts and architectural drawings. This polished businessman was so different from the wild teenager she'd known. Yet something in the way he stood, the slight tilt of his head when he made a point, was exactly the same.

Miss Eleanor's fingers drummed against the armrest of her chair, a subtle sign of her displeasure. Rachel Masters furiously scribbled notes beside them while Tim Marshall nodded enthusiastically with each of Cliff's points from across the aisle.

Tim stepped up to the microphone first after Cliff's presentation. Beverly had known Tim since high school. His family had lived on the island for three generations.

"This development could bring fresh life to our town," Tim said. "My son wants to stay here, but there aren't enough opportunities for young people. This project could change that."

A few more people stepped up. Each voiced

support for the project, painting pictures of a thriving future with more jobs and tourists.

Her chest grew heavy as she listened. Just two weeks ago, these same people had gathered at Coastal Coffee for the annual Small Business Saturday celebration. They'd laughed together, shared stories, and helped decorate the street. Now the room crackled with tension as supporters and opponents sat divided.

Greg Wark, the marina owner, stood up next. "The hotel will bring year-round visitors, not just summer tourists. That means steady business for all of us."

More nods of agreement rippled through one side of the room while frowns deepened on the other. She remembered when town meetings meant working together to plan festivals or organize beach cleanups. The sense of unity that had always defined Magnolia Key felt like it was slipping away.

Miss Eleanor rose from her seat, her movements deliberate and graceful. She made her way to the microphone. The room fell silent.

"I've lived on this island for seventy-five years," she began. "That boardwalk property you want to develop? My grandfather helped build it. The original pilings still stand there, cut from island pine trees." Her voice carried clearly through the room. "Every summer, families gather there to watch the sunset. Children learn to fish off those boards, just like their parents and grandparents did."

Miss Eleanor's gaze found Cliff's face. "My son seems to have forgotten that some things are worth more than money. That spot holds generations of memories for island families. Progress doesn't have to mean destroying our heritage."

She watched Cliff closely during his mother's speech. His expression remained neutral, but she noticed the muscle working in his jaw. It was the exact same tell he'd had as a teenager when he was angry but trying not to show it. His hands gripped the edge of the table where he sat, his knuckles white with tension.

Miss Eleanor wasn't finished. "The Whitmores have always protected this island's character. We've been its guardians since the first settler stepped ashore." She paused, her eyes still locked with Cliff's. "I expected better from a Whitmore heir."

The disappointment in Miss Eleanor's voice cut through the room. Cliff's jaw clenched tighter, but he didn't look away from her steady gaze. Miss Eleanor turned to return to her seat.

Beverly stood, and her heart pounded as she approached the microphone. Her hands shook slightly as she adjusted it to her height. She took a deep breath, trying to calm her nerves. Public speaking had never been her strong suit, but this was too important to stay silent.

"Magnolia Key is a special place," she began, wondering if everyone could hear the slight tremble in her voice. "It's not just the beautiful beaches or the quaint shops. It's the feeling you get when you walk down the street and everyone knows your name. The way the community comes together for festivals and potlucks. It's the sense of history that lingers in every old building and weathered dock."

She glanced at Cliff, but his expression was unreadable, even for her. "This proposed development would forever change the character of our town. That stretch of boardwalk is where generations have gathered to watch the sunset, to fish, to make memories. Replacing it with a high-rise would alter the very skyline that defines Magnolia Key."

Her voice grew steadier as she continued. "I understand the desire for progress, for economic growth. But at what cost? Do we want to sacrifice the charm and heritage that make our town unique? Do we want to become just another beach town, overdeveloped and indistinguishable from a dozen others up and down the coast? Once we change our building codes and allow this one building, are more to come?"

She paused, looking out at the faces of her neighbors. "Magnolia Key is more than just a place. It's a community, a family. And like any family, we won't always agree. But I hope we can find a way to move forward together, to grow and thrive without losing the essence of who we are."

She turned to Cliff. "Go stand on that boardwalk. Think about what it will be like to not even be able to see the ocean from there with the high-rise blocking the view."

This time, she could read his face. He was thinking about the times they both went out there to watch the sunset. But he quickly recovered and his neutral expression settled back on his features.

As she stepped back from the microphone, her legs felt shaky. She returned to her seat beside Miss Eleanor, who patted her hand approvingly.

The mayor called for the next speaker, and a man Beverly recognized as a local contractor stepped up. "With all due respect, Miss Mooney," he began, "Magnolia Key can't survive on charm alone. We need jobs, we need industry. This development could be the shot in the arm our economy needs."

From across the aisle, Sarah Smith stood up. "At the expense of our history? Our environment? There are other ways to bring jobs without destroying the character of the town."

The contractor shook his head. "Easy for you to say when your livelihood doesn't depend on growth. Some of us are barely hanging on. We need this project."

More voices joined in, the room growing louder

as people shouted over each other to be heard. The mayor banged his gavel, trying to restore order, but the damage was done. The division in the room was unmistakable, a chasm that seemed to grow wider with each heated exchange. It seemed like the very fabric of their community was unraveling, torn apart by conflicting visions of the future.

She caught Cliff's eye across the room. For a moment, she saw a flicker of the boy she'd once known, the one who loved this island as fiercely as she did. Then his expression hardened, and he looked away.

The mayor finally managed to quiet the crowd. "We will have order," he said sternly. "Everyone will have a chance to speak. But we will do so respectfully. Let's give Mr. Griffin a chance to speak again."

She watched as Cliff stood, straightening his tie before returning to the podium. His shoulders were relaxed, and he carried himself with an easy confidence. A confidence he'd tried to portray when they were younger, but she'd known the insecure boy under his bravado. But his confidence now was sincere and polished, refined by years of business dealings.

His eyes met hers briefly before he looked away. She felt that familiar flutter in her chest, the one she'd been fighting since he returned to town.

"This project isn't about erasing Magnolia Key's

past," he said. "It's about securing its future while honoring its heritage. We can preserve what makes this place special while creating opportunities for the next generation. This is one way to do it. When the bridge is finished, more people will find your—*our*—town. We need to rise to the challenge and provide for them."

The crowd erupted into heated discussion again, their voices rising steadily. Some pointed at the renderings, while others gestured emphatically at their neighbors. The division in the room grew more apparent with each passing moment.

Miss Eleanor rose again, her spine straight as a rail. "Mr. Mayor, I have more to say about this matter."

"I'm sorry, Miss Eleanor. The rules clearly state one comment per person. We need to give everyone a chance to speak." The mayor's tone was respectful but firm.

Miss Eleanor settled back into her seat, her lips pressed into a thin line. Beverly recognized the signs of her building frustration. The woman who usually commanded any room she entered had been silenced.

She glanced at Cliff, who stood near his presentation boards, arms crossed as he observed the room. His expression remained neutral, but she recognized the slight tension in his shoulders. He'd always carried his stress there, even as a teenager.

"This isn't right," Miss Eleanor muttered beside her. "They need to hear the whole story."

The crowd's volume increased further. Old friends who usually shared coffee and conversation at her shop now sat in opposing camps, their faces set in determined lines. The room felt smaller somehow, compressed by the conflicting hopes and fears for their town's future.

The mayor banged his gavel again, quieting the crowd. "I think we've heard enough for now. We'll turn all this over to the planning committee and they'll take all your comments under advisement. Then they'll make their decision. Meeting adjourned."

Beverly rose from her seat. For now, all she could do was listen as her neighbors continued to argue, their voices rising and falling like the tide. She prayed that somehow they would find a way to bridge the divide and preserve what made Magnolia Key special while still allowing room for growth. The alternative—a town torn apart by discord and resentment—was too painful to contemplate.

CHAPTER 4

Beverly wiped down the counter one last time as the lunch crowd thinned out. Only a few tables remained, lingering over their coffee. Maxine had stayed to help clean up, though Beverly suspected she had ulterior motives.

"Come sit with me," Maxine called from their usual corner table. "That counter won't get any cleaner."

She set down her cloth and joined her friend. The table was ready for tomorrow's guests, with the salt and pepper shakers full and a small bowl of artificial sugar and creamer sitting beside them. She focused on adjusting shakers until they were perfectly lined up with the sugar shaker.

"So." Maxine's voice held that gentle, prodding tone she knew too well. "Are we going to talk about it?"

"Talk about what?" She adjusted the shakers again.

"About how you nearly dropped that entire tray of mugs when you saw Cliff walk past the window this morning."

"I did not." But she had come close.

"Beverly." Maxine waited until she looked up. "How are you really feeling about him being back?"

"I don't know what you mean."

"Yes, you do. Talk to me."

"I'm angry. So angry." Her voice came out tight, strained. "But then I see the way Eleanor tears into him in public, and I remember that lost little boy who could never do anything right." She sighed as she ran her fingers along the edge of the table. "I feel angry, but I also… I can't help feeling sorry for him."

Maxine waited for her to continue.

"Remember that science fair disaster?" She closed her eyes, remembering twelve-year-old Cliff standing in front of his project. He'd worked so hard on it, determined to win first place. To make his parents proud. But something went wrong with his volcano experiment, and instead of a controlled eruption, it sprayed red foam all over the gym floor. Eleanor had pressed her lips together in that way she had while his father had simply walked away.

She shook her head. "Or that spelling bee in

eighth grade. He studied every night for a month. He was so sure he would win."

"But he froze on stage," Maxine finished. "I remember."

"His father didn't even stay to watch. Said he had a meeting." Her throat tightened at the memory. "Eleanor sat there with her spine straight as a board, but you could see the disappointment in her eyes. And Cliff… he tried so hard to act like it didn't matter."

Maxine reached across the table and squeezed her hand. "He was always trying to get their attention, wasn't he? Even when he was causing trouble."

"Especially then. At least when he was in trouble, they had to notice him."

The familiar chime of the door interrupted them and her fingers froze on the sugar shaker as Cliff stepped inside, dressed in crisp navy slacks and a light blue button-down that seemed too formal for her casual cafe. His polished appearance was another reminder of how far he'd come from that boy who used to show up at her door in worn jeans and a faded T-shirt.

The usual afternoon chatter died down as several regulars turned to stare. Mrs. Henderson set her coffee cup down with a clatter. Tony's newspaper rustled as he lowered it to watch. Even

Janine, who'd been wiping tables, paused with her cloth suspended in midair.

Her chest tightened. This was her space. Her cafe. The one place she'd carved out for herself after all these years. She'd built it from nothing, turned it into somewhere people felt at home. Somewhere she felt at home.

She pushed back her chair and stood, her movement sharp and decisive. "Didn't I ask you to find a different place to eat?"

Her voice carried across the quiet restaurant, harder than she'd meant it to be. She saw Mrs. Henderson's eyebrows shoot up, and Tony's mouth dropped open slightly. She never spoke to customers that way. Everyone knew Beverly Mooney treated each person who walked through her door like family.

Cliff stopped in the middle of the floor, one hand still gripping the strap of his leather briefcase. For just a moment, his confident expression slipped. She caught a flicker of something in his eyes. That same hurt she used to see when his father would dismiss his achievements with a wave of his hand, or when Eleanor would purse her lips and say, "Well, I suppose that's the best you could do."

The look vanished so quickly she might have imagined it, replaced by that smooth mask he wore now. But she knew what she'd seen. She'd spent years watching him hide his pain behind a smile, pretending nothing could touch him.

Maxine's hand brushed her arm, a gentle reminder that they weren't alone, that this moment was playing out in front of an audience. But she couldn't seem to move, caught between the woman she was now and the girl who'd once promised to meet him at the ferry dock, her heart full of dreams that had been shattered.

Her hands clenched at her sides as he strode past her and up to the counter, his polished shoes clicking against the wooden floor. He kept his gaze fixed on the menu board above, though she knew he'd never needed to look at it. He'd ordered the same thing since high school. Black coffee, two sugars. That was back before she'd bought the shop and renovated it and made it into what it was today. Hers.

"Large coffee, two sugars." He paused and glanced at her before turning back to the counter. "To go," he said to no one in particular, his voice carrying that practiced smoothness she'd come to associate with this new grown-up version of Cliff. The successful developer. A man so different from the boy who used to gulp down his coffee and tell her wild stories about his plans for the future.

The silence in the cafe pressed in around them. Everyone watched, waiting. Mrs. Henderson hadn't touched her coffee since Cliff walked in. Tony's newspaper lay forgotten on his table.

Janine darted forward, her movements jerky as she reached for a cup, her hands trembling. The girl's gaze kept bouncing between Beverly and Cliff like she was watching a tennis match, waiting for the next serve.

"I can handle this," Beverly said, but Janine had already grabbed the coffeepot.

"No, no, I've got it," Janine insisted, her voice pitched higher than usual. She turned too quickly, and coffee sloshed over the rim of the pot onto the counter.

Of course. Janine was always dropping or spilling something, but the girl had a heart of gold and was a hard worker.

"Oh! Sorry, sorry." She grabbed a cloth and dabbed at the spill, nearly knocking over the stack of cups in her haste.

Beverly stepped forward to help, but Cliff's presence at the counter stopped her. He stood there like he belonged. Like he hadn't walked away from this town—from her—all those years ago. Like he wasn't trying to change everything about the place she'd built her life around.

Janine finally managed to pour his coffee, only spilling a little more in the process. Her hands shook as she added the sugar, stirring so vigorously that coffee splashed onto the counter.

"Here you go, Mr. Griffin." Janine plopped a top on the cup and pushed it toward him. She glanced at Beverly again, her expression uncertain.

He reached for his wallet, still refusing to look in her direction. The leather looked expensive. Everything about him seemed expensive now. His clothes, his briefcase, even the way he held himself. It was all carefully crafted to project success.

The cafe remained unusually quiet. Usually, at this time, there'd be the gentle murmur of conversation, the rustle of newspapers, the clink of spoons against coffee cups. But now there was just the sound of Janine's nervous breathing and the soft whir of the ceiling fans.

She watched as he placed a twenty on the counter. "Keep the change," he said to Janine, who broke into a wide smile as she snatched up the bill.

She wanted to tell him to take his money and leave. Wanted to tell him that she didn't need his generous tips or his development plans or anything else from him.

Janine hovered nearby, wiping the same spot on the counter over and over, her cloth moving in increasingly frantic circles.

The sudden crackle of static from the radio behind the counter cut through the tension. She'd never put in a fancy sound system, instead enjoying the normal radio broadcasts. The soft music that had been playing faded into silence, replaced by the urgent voice of the broadcaster.

"We interrupt our regular programming to bring you this weather alert. That hurricane we've all been watching for the last week and hoping would settle down has picked up in intensity. And it's made a surprising turn that not many of the models had expected. The National Hurricane Center has issued a hurricane warning for the following counties…"

Her attention snapped to the radio as the announcer listed their county among others. She'd lived on Magnolia Key long enough to know that tone. Knew that carefully measured voice that tried to convey urgency without causing panic.

"Hurricane Camille has shifted course and is now expected to make landfall along the southwestern coast of Florida. Current projections show the storm reaching category two and possibly three strength before impact."

The coffee cup in Cliff's hand remained suspended halfway to his mouth. Around the cafe, conversations stopped. Papers lowered. Heads turned toward the radio.

"Residents in coastal areas should begin preparation immediately. Heavy rainfall of up to ten inches expected."

Her mind kicked into preparation mode. If it was headed this way, she needed to board up the windows. Move everything inside. Check her generator. Call her supplier to cancel deliveries for later in the week. The mental checklist grew with each passing second.

She caught Maxine's eye across the room. Her friend's face mirrored her own concern. They'd been through storms before, but category three was not one to ignore. That was serious.

"All residents should be prepared for extended power outages and limited access to emergency services. It is highly suggested that people on the outer islands consider evacuating. Mandatory evacuation orders will be coming as we know more."

The radio continued with more details of wind speeds, precipitation estimates, and storm surge predictions. But her thoughts raced ahead to what needed to be done. The cafe's windows weren't impact-resistant. She'd meant to upgrade them last year, but kept putting it off. She could use the old hurricane shutters again. The storage room had supplies from the last storm, but she needed to check what was still good.

"Maxine," she said, her voice cutting through the radio's drone. "Help me check the hurricane kit?"

"Of course." Maxine stood, already moving toward the storage room.

The other customers began gathering their

things, their movements carrying the hurried energy of people who suddenly had too much to do and too little time. Tony folded his newspaper with quick, sharp movements. Mrs. Henderson fumbled in her purse for her phone, likely calling her daughter on the mainland.

She glanced at the wall of windows facing the street. The sky still looked deceptively peaceful, showing no hint of the chaos heading their way. But she knew how quickly that could change. She'd seen sunny mornings turn into howling tempests often enough growing up here.

She turned back toward the storage room, nearly colliding with Cliff, who still stood near the counter, his coffee forgotten in his hand. For a moment, their earlier tension seemed to hover between them, but then he set down his cup.

"Can I do anything?"

"No, I've got it."

The radio droned on with evacuation routes and emergency shelter locations, but she turned her focus to what needed doing. She had a lot to do and not much time to do it.

CHAPTER 5

Eleanor and Jonah stood on her front porch. Jonah had already hauled her hurricane shutters to the porch, leaning them against the railings. She usually hired out any hurricane preparations, but her usual handyman was swamped this time now that the hurricane had changed its course and was headed their direction. Jonah had insisted on putting up the shutters for her.

"I'm glad I got the top floors outfitted with hurricane windows. At least you won't have to climb up high to hang the shutters up there. I'm scheduled to have the rest of the windows replaced, but they won't be in for another month or so." Eleanor scowled. "Should have gotten them all done at the same time."

"It's no problem, Ellie. I already have the shutters up at my place. Helps that my place is just one story, and one of the previous owners put up accordion hurricane blinds."

"I just have these horrible shutters that need to be screwed into place. It's a lot of work."

Jonah picked up the drill. "Don't worry about it. I'll have them up in no time."

She glanced over at her dog, Winston, who was pacing the porch. "Winston is always a bit nervous when a hurricane is coming. He senses them."

Jonah reached down and petted Winston's head. "It's okay, buddy."

Eleanor looked up, surprised to see Cliff pull his fancy car up to the curb. Her fingers gripped the porch railing. Winston stopped his pacing and sat beside her, his tail thumping against the wooden boards.

"Mother." Her son strode up the walkway, his expensive shoes clicking against the pavement. His suit looked out of place on Magnolia Key. Always had to dress to impress. Even in a hurricane.

She tapped her fingers on the railing. "Cliff."

"Mr. Burton." Cliff nodded to Jonah, who had paused in his work on the shutters.

"Cliff." Jonah's response was polite but cool.

Cliff started to speak again, but she held up her hand. "If you've come to give me your unwelcomed opinion again about me dating Jonah, you can just turn around and leave."

"No, Mother. You've made it perfectly clear you don't want my opinion." He looked over at Jonah. "I just want you to… be careful."

"Cliff…" she warned.

He held up his hands. "Anyway, that's not why I'm here. I came to check if you needed help preparing for the hurricane."

"As you can see, Jonah is helping me. I don't need your help."

Winston stood and walked over to Cliff, tail wagging. Traitor.

Cliff bent down to pet Winston. "Hey, old boy. How are you doing?"

"He's fine. Though the hurricane makes him nervous."

"Just like Murphy, remember him?"

Of course, she remembered Murphy, her very first cavalier.

"I remember how he used to hide under my bed during storms when he was a puppy."

She did remember that. Murphy would scratch at Cliff's door until he let him in. Her son had been so patient with Murphy. One of the few things he'd done right in her opinion.

"Well, since you can see I'm taken care of, you can go now." She waved her hand in dismissal.

"But I was hoping to talk to you about the development project—"

"No." Winston looked up at her, surprised at her sharp tone, and hurried over to her side.

Cliff straightened, his jaw clenched. "Fine. But I'm not giving up on the project."

"I wouldn't expect anything less from you. You never did listen to anyone else's opinions."

Cliff stalked down the walkway and slid into his car. Its engine sprang to life smoothly, unlike her old car that always had to protest a bit before starting for her.

As Cliff's car disappeared down the street, her fingers still gripped the porch railing. Winston pressed against her leg, offering his silent support, his brown eyes looking up at her with what seemed like an apology for letting Cliff pet him.

Jonah set down the drill and walked over to her. "Are you all right?"

"Yes." She paused, releasing her grip on the railing. "No." She turned to face him. "I'm just so disappointed in my son. In what he's become. I keep thinking that someday he'll be... different."

She sank into one of the white rocking chairs on her porch. Winston settled at her feet and rested his head on her shoes.

"He's still your son," Jonah said, taking the chair beside her. "Maybe he really believes this project will help Magnolia Key grow."

She shook her head. "No. This is about money. Or showing off to the town how successful he's become." She gazed down the street where his car had disappeared. "Did you see that suit? Those shoes? That ridiculous car? Everything about him screams that he needs everyone to know how well he's done for himself."

"Could be. Or maybe he's looking for acceptance from the town."

"Acceptance?" She let out a dry laugh. "By destroying what makes this place special? By trying to turn us into every other overdeveloped beach town?" Her fingers found their way to the arm of the rocker, tapping out her frustration.

"I'm just saying, sometimes people go about things the wrong way when they're trying to prove themselves."

"Well, this certainly isn't the way to get acceptance. Not from me. Not from anyone who truly loves this town." She looked over at Jonah. "You've only been back her a short while, but you understand what makes Magnolia Key special. The sense of community. The way we look out for each other."

"I do. But I also understand wanting to make your mark. To show people you've changed."

"Changed?" She snorted. "Cliff hasn't changed at all. He's still that same selfish boy who only thinks about what he wants."

Winston lifted his head at her sharp tone, and she reached down to scratch behind his ears.

"I'm sorry," she said, softening her voice. "I know you're trying to help. To see both sides. But I've had years of watching Cliff do whatever suited him best. Years of hoping he'd grow into the kind of man who would make me proud. Instead, he comes back here with his fancy car and his big plans, ready to tear down everything we've built."

Jonah reached over and placed his hand over hers, stilling her tapping fingers. "You're allowed to be angry with him. To disagree with his choices. But don't let it eat you up inside."

She turned her hand over to squeeze his briefly before standing up. "I suppose we should finish with these shutters before the weather turns."

Jonah stood up beside her. "Okay, but one more thing, Ellie."

She paused and looked at him. "What?"

"You don't have to protect me from what Cliff thinks or says about me. I'm sure other people in town are wondering the same thing he is."

She looked up at Jonah's weathered face, seeing the genuine concern in his eyes. "What do they wonder?"

"What you see in me." His voice was soft, gentle.

She reached up and touched his face, her fingers

tracing the lines etched around his eyes, signs of shared laughter from decades past. "I see a very kind man. A man who I was a fool to walk away from all those years ago, before I understood what truly mattered."

CHAPTER 6

Beverly watched as Dale entered Coastal Coffee, a warm smile lighting up his face when he spotted Maxine behind the counter. Her best friend's eyes sparkled as she looked up from where she was restocking coffee cups.

"Hey there, beautiful," Dale said, walking over to give Maxine a quick kiss.

Beverly busied herself wiping down a nearby table, giving them a moment of privacy, but she was still unable to keep from smiling. After everything Maxine had been through with her ex-husband, Victor, seeing her friend so happy made Beverly's heart full. Dale took Maxine's hand when she came out from behind the counter. They fit together naturally, at ease with each other. He brought out a lightness in Maxine that she hadn't seen in years.

Dale led Maxine over to where Beverly was pretending to be busy. "So, I have some news."

She looked up and grinned. "Tell me the hurricane is turning away from us."

He flashed a wry smile. "I wish I could say that. No, it's about Vera and Prince Lawrence."

"Oh, you found out something new?"

"I think so. I have to do some more digging before I share my news with Miss Eleanor—"

"Beverly!" Darlene burst through the door of Coastal Coffee, breathless. She hurried over to them. "Did you hear? Mandatory evacuations for the island."

She did a quick appraisal of the shop. They'd boarded up most of the windows except the front one so she could keep serving people. But now, it was time to shut it all down.

"The ferry's running extra trips to get folks off the island, but the last ferry will run tomorrow about sunset," Darlene continued, fanning herself with a menu she'd grabbed from a nearby table. "We got to hurry and finish battening down the hatches. My goodness, I still have half the B&B to secure, and those shutters are heavy. Luckily, Felicity and Brent are in town, and Mark is helping me too."

Dale reached out and touched Beverly's arm. "Let me help you finish with the hurricane shutters for the cafe. I already have Second Finds boarded up. Not many people looking for antiques with the storm approaching."

"Thanks, I'll take you up on that." She nodded gratefully.

Darlene turned to leave. "Just wanted to make sure you heard. And I need a few things from the hardware store. They'll be closing soon, I'm sure. Then I've got to get back to the B&B."

"Thanks, Darlene. Stay safe." She walked her to the door and turned to the remaining customers. "I'm sure you heard. Let's get finished up here, and I'll close up."

Her customers hurried to finish up and pay as Dale and Maxine worked on putting up the hurricane shutters over the front window, plunging the cafe into an unfamiliar dimness barely illuminated by the lights. Coastal Coffee was supposed to be filled with light and… well, there wasn't time to think about that.

Maxine came back in, and they rinsed the dishes, leaving them in the sink. Beverly took one last glance around the kitchen, making sure everything was secure. It wasn't the first time she'd had to leave the cafe for an evacuation, but it never got any easier.

The three of them walked out of the cafe, and Dale peered down the street. "You know, I want one last check of Second Finds." He gave Maxine a quick kiss. "I'll meet you back at my cottage in a bit?"

"I'm going to go with Beverly and help her finish closing up her cottage." Maxine turned to her. "Because I know you've put all your energy into making sure that Coastal Coffee was secure, and knowing you, you haven't finished with your cottage."

She laughed. "You know me too well. I still need to drag the outside planters in. I have a few more shutters to put up. I hate not having any natural light inside, so I left off the two in the kitchen."

"You both stay safe." Dale gave Maxine another kiss and hurried down the street.

"I'd almost forgotten about all the prep for possible hurricanes. Pushed it from my memory, I guess." Maxine fell into step beside her.

"It's been a while since we've had a big one. But Magnolia Key has weathered the storms before. We'll get through this one."

As they reached the cottage, she pulled out her keys and opened the front door. She flipped on the light in the dark room. "See, I hate this about the shutters. So dark inside."

Maxine helped her put up the last shutters, and they hurried to bring in everything from outside. They carried in the porch furniture and planters and set them in the entranceway.

"Do you have your to-go bag packed?"

"I do. Important files. A photo album from Mama. I keep meaning to scan the pages in so I'd never lose the photos, but I haven't made time. And I have a few mementos that I'd hate to lose."

Maxine grinned at her. "Did you remember to pack clothes?"

"Yes, those too." She grinned as she rubbed her back, exhausted. "I have some tea in the fridge. Want a glass and a quick sit before you head home?"

"That sounds wonderful." Maxine sat down with a sigh. "All this preparation has me thinking about when we were kids during that one hurricane. Mabel? Carol? Whatever the name. We were just in grade school and so scared. Do you remember how your mother made us play cards and drink hot chocolate to distract us?"

She brought the glasses to the table and sat next to her friend. "How could I forget? You cried the entire time, convinced the storm surge would sweep us all away."

"I was a dramatic kid," Maxine admitted, a sheepish grin spreading across her face. "But you have to admit, it was a pretty scary storm. Remember the old oak tree near Miss Eleanor's? It split right down the middle, and I thought it was the end of the world."

"Miss Eleanor was annoyed. Said the tree had been there for years and the storm had no right to destroy it." She smiled, remembering. "I think Miss Eleanor was offended it dared to split like that. In *her* yard."

"But it came back, didn't it? Stronger than ever."

"It did." She nodded, thinking of how beautiful the tree was in front of Miss Eleanor's house now.

"I wonder how Miss Eleanor is doing with this hurricane."

"I'm sure Jonah is helping her secure her house."

Maxine leaned forward. "Isn't that great that they found each other again after all this time?"

"It is. And have you heard him call her Ellie?" She grinned. "I think that's adorable."

Maxine took one last sip of tea and stood. "I should get home. Dale helped me get everything secured already, but I'd like one last look. I think we'll head out on the first ferry tomorrow."

"That's my plan too. They'll probably run extra ferries, but they'll have to stop when the bay gets rough from the approaching storm."

She walked her friend to the front door and stepped outside with her. The sky was still a crystal clear blue with just a few clouds dotting the expanse. She hugged Maxine. "Stay safe. I'll catch up with you on the mainland."

Maxine hurried off down the street. As she turned to go inside, she caught sight of a familiar figure hurrying up the path, his face etched with concern.

"Cliff." He was the last thing she needed now.

"Beverly, hi. I just wanted to make sure you heard about the mandatory evacuation orders."

"I did." Her words were clipped.

"Can I help with anything? Carry things in? Hang shutters?"

"It's all done." Not that she would have accepted help from him anyway.

"You sure? There's nothing I can do?"

"Oh, I think you've done enough for this town." She swirled around and walked inside, leaving him standing on her porch.

CHAPTER 7

Cliff stood on Beverly's porch, staring at the closed door. Same old Beverly. Same old town. No one wanted his help. Not even when he genuinely offered it, with no strings attached.

He turned and walked to his car as irritation surged through him. Why did she always insist on handling everything herself? It was just like dealing with his mother all over again. Another stubborn Magnolia Key woman pushing him away when all he wanted to do was help.

He slipped into his car to head over to his mother's house. She always treated evacuation orders like optional suggestions, no matter how serious the warning. He'd call to check on her, but she never answered her cell phone. Said she didn't need it since everyone knew where to find her.

He parked his car and got out. Winston greeted

him with a lazy wag of his tail as he climbed the porch steps. He lifted the brass door knocker and let it go, hearing it echo through the hallway.

His mother's deliberate footsteps sounded through the door before she opened it and stood there, her back straight and a disapproving look on her face. "Cliff, I thought you'd be off the island by now."

"I just wanted to check on you. Make sure you heard about the mandatory evacuation. When are you leaving?" He eyed her suspiciously. "You are leaving, right?"

"I'm aware of the evacuation orders and I'm perfectly capable of making my own decision about leaving my home—or not."

"Mother, you can't stay here during a hurricane."

"It's only going to be a category two, maybe three at most. Winston and I will be fine."

"You're leaving." He stepped into the foyer. "Remember that category three we rode out? The one where you insisted we should stay? The one where half the roof came off? And the hurricane shutters tore off the big window and rain poured in?"

"That was different. And the house has new hurricane windows now. Well, at least upstairs." She paused and looked at him sharply. "We've been through storms before, and we'll weather this one."

She spoke as if that ended the entire discussion. As if she could control a hurricane through sheer Whitmore stubbornness.

Jonah appeared behind her, nodding a greeting, a look of relief briefly crossing his features. "I was just trying to convince Ellie we need to head to the mainland." Jonah shook his head. "She hasn't exactly been cooperative."

"I'm more than cooperative," she protested sharply. "I just see no point in panicking. The forecast keeps shifting back and forth—first it's a two, then maybe a three, then back to a two. Those weather reporters haven't got a clue. We've lived through worse. Cliff, you know that well enough."

He met her gaze. "Mother, I know you take pride in being stubborn. But there's a fine line between stubborn and reckless. Will you really risk your safety—all because you refuse to listen to common sense?"

"I won't have you lecturing me on common sense. Common sense says that you'd realize your ridiculous development is a poor idea for the town."

He let out a long sigh. It always came back to him screwing things up as far as his mother was concerned.

"And both of you can stop treating me like I'm some helpless old woman. I've lived through plenty of storms. This is my home. You two feel free to leave if you're concerned. But I'm not going anywhere."

"I'm not leaving you, Ellie." Jonah put a hand on her shoulder.

"Your home will still be here when you get back." At least he hoped it would. You never knew with these hurricanes.

Jonah turned and looked patiently at his mother. With way more patience than he had for her. "Ellie, we really don't want to put any rescue workers at risk if we stay here and need help, do we?"

She stared at Jonah for a moment. "Fine. But only because you already made arrangements at a nice hotel a bit inland." She pointed her finger at Cliff. "Not because you told me to. We'll leave in the morning. No use wasting money on a hotel room tonight."

Relief swept through him. She'd finally listened to reason. "Do you need help getting your things together?"

"No, I'm perfectly capable of packing." She waved her hand at him. "You can go now."

"Mother—"

She turned and headed for the stairs. "I'm sure you have other things to do. Development plans to work on. Buildings to design that will ruin our town."

"Ellie," Jonah said softly. "Now is not the time…"

She paused on the third step. "You're right. I need to pack." She continued up the stairs without looking back.

He stood there, feeling like that teenage boy who could never do anything right.

Jonah clasped his shoulder. "Thanks for the reinforcements. Your mother is a stubborn one. Always has been." He smiled. "But I wouldn't have her any other way. We'll leave on the first ferry in the morning. I'll make sure she gets to the hotel."

"Thanks." He headed for the door. "Text me when you get there."

"Will do."

He walked out, and Winston followed him to the porch. The old dog wagged his tail as Cliff scratched behind his ears. "Take care of her, boy."

He headed to his car and drove back into town. Most of the shops had their hurricane shutters up, but he spotted Patty Miller struggling with a large piece of plywood outside of her gift shop.

He pulled into an empty parking spot and got out. "Need some help with that?"

Patty looked up, her hair blowing around her face. "Oh, Cliff. Yes, actually. I keep forgetting how much work it is to board everything up."

He took the plywood from her and positioned it over the window. "Got a drill?"

"Right here." She handed him the power tool.

"Thank you. I wasn't sure how I was going to manage this by myself."

"Happy to help." He secured the plywood. "How many more windows do you need to cover?"

"Just the side window. I've got the back done already."

They worked together to get the final window covered. Patty stood back and eyed the window with a satisfied smile. "I really appreciate your help."

"No problem. Anyone else need help?"

"I think Sarah at the bookstore was having trouble with her shutters. The track's a bit rusty."

He nodded and headed down the street to the bookstore. Sarah stood outside, yanking on a metal shutter that refused to budge.

"Want me to take a look at that?"

She glanced over her shoulder. "Oh. Well, I suppose."

He examined the track. "Just needs some WD-40. Got any?"

"Inside." She disappeared into the shop and returned with a can.

A few sprays of lubricant and the shutter slid smoothly closed. He helped her with the remaining windows, then moved on to the next shop.

Some owners accepted his help readily. Others declined, saying they had it under control or help was already on the way. A few just shook their heads and went inside when they saw him approach.

He spied Mrs. Carson trying to load supplies into her car.

"Here, let me get that for you." He lifted the boxes easily and placed them in her trunk.

"Thank you, Cliff." She patted his arm. "You were always such a strong boy. Remember when you helped build that ramp for my granddad's wheelchair?"

"That was a long time ago."

"Still, you did good things back then. And you're doing good things now, helping folks prepare." She got into her car. "Sometimes people forget the good parts."

He watched her drive away, thinking about her words. The sun was getting low, and the street was growing empty. A string of boarded-up shops lined the street. He'd done what he could.

He'd head to the mainland himself first thing in the morning. Though part of him wanted to stay, to prove to everyone he did care about this town. But that would just be foolish. And they probably wouldn't believe him, anyway.

CHAPTER 8

Beverly stepped out onto her front porch, keys gripped tightly in her hand. She'd gone through her mental checklist three times now. Windows secured. Photos packed. Insurance documents tucked safely in her bag. Computer in the car. Other important items placed in waterproof containers and set up high.

Dark clouds churned above as she turned back for one final look through the open door. The house felt different. It felt empty and vulnerable, like it knew what was coming. Her home for over twenty years stood waiting, braced for whatever the hurricane decided to throw at it.

"Please still be here when I get back," she whispered, then pulled the door closed and locked it. The metal hurricane shutters clanked as she secured them across the front door.

The palm trees beside the house were already dancing in the wind with this outer band of storms kicked up by the hurricane. She hurried to her car and shoved in the last bag she carried.

She should go straight to the ferry, but she couldn't stop the urge to drive past Coastal Coffee for one last look. She only passed one car. No people walking dogs or jogging. No kids on bikes. Just bare streets and locked-up buildings. A plastic chair someone had forgotten to secure tumbled down the street.

She slowed as she approached her shop. A closed for storm sign hung in the window. All the furniture had been moved inside. Hurricane shutters covered every window. She'd done everything she could to protect it.

Memories of past storms flickered through her mind. The time the front window shattered during Hurricane Matthew, the water damage from Irma that took months to repair, and the week without power after Andrew. Each time they'd rebuilt, but it never got easier leaving, not knowing what she'd find when she returned.

With one last look, she headed to the ferry landing. The line for the ferry stretched back several blocks. Cars crept forward slowly as more island residents joined the evacuation. Beverly fell into line behind Mrs. Peterson's blue Buick. Up ahead, she could see the ferry loading vehicles.

The radio crackled with updates about the hurricane's path. Category three now, possibly strengthening to a four. Mandatory evacuations expanded.

She inched forward with the line of cars. So many familiar faces in the vehicles around her, all looking as worried as she felt. Rain began to splatter on her windshield.

After she finally made it onto the ferry, she made her way up to the passenger deck like she usually did, but this time, she chose the enclosed section instead of standing out at the railing like she preferred.

She threaded her way through the clusters of people gathered on the covered part of the passenger deck, many with worried expressions as they gazed back toward Magnolia Key. She recognized most of the faces—neighbors, customers, friends—all evacuating like her.

The sound of the ferry's horn cut through the thickening air, piercing the anxiety hanging over the crowd, as if to remind them of the reality of their departure. The mournful tone lingered in the air, a bittersweet farewell to the island.

"Beverly! Over here!"

She turned at the familiar voice and spotted Maxine waving at her from the railing. Dale stood beside her, one arm protectively around her shoulders. A wave of relief washed over her as she made her way toward them.

"I was hoping I'd find you two," she said, joining them at the window. "Traffic's terrible. I was wondering if you'd made it to the ferry."

"Barely," Dale said. "We were one of the last cars they let on. A lot of residents left yesterday, but it appears quite a few waited until today."

Her heart ached as she turned to look back at Magnolia Key. The island grew smaller with each passing minute, its familiar silhouette shrinking against the darkening sky. The normally picturesque view was marred by ominous clouds building on the horizon. A lone sunbeam tried to slash its way through the clouds, illuminating the churning water in the bay for just a moment before the clouds closed around it.

"Did you get everything secured?" Maxine's brow creased with concern.

"I think so. And thanks for the help yesterday. I finished up all the usual preparations. Still doesn't make it any easier to leave." She gripped the railing. "All these years of hurricanes, and it never gets easier."

"Lived inland most of my life, and I still dread these storms. The antiques at the store are all elevated and covered. Did what I could." Dale stared across the water.

The three stood quietly for a moment, watching

their home recede into the distance. The wind picked up, whipping her hair across her face. She tucked it behind her ear and zipped her jacket higher.

"You two staying in Weston?" she asked.

"Yes. I haven't forgotten the town tradition of people trying to book hotels in that area on the western edge of Fort Lauderdale. I expect most people will be there if they don't have family or friends to stay with." Maxine leaned closer against Dale, who drew her tightly to his side. "We're at the Marriott. Were you able to get a reservation there too?"

"I did. It's about two and a half hours east if traffic's normal. Which it won't be." She shook her head. "Will probably take us hours and hours."

The ferry's horn blasted again, making them all jump. She watched as the last visible outlines of Magnolia Key disappeared from view. Her chest tightened. She'd left her home before, but this time felt different. Maybe because of all the changes already happening on the island—Cliff's return, his development plans, the town's division. And now this storm threatening to rewrite everything again.

"Think Jonah convinced Miss Eleanor to leave?" Maxine asked, breaking into Beverly's thoughts.

"I hope so. That woman is stubborn as they come," she replied. "But Jonah seems to have a way with her that nobody else does."

"What about…" Maxine hesitated, glancing sideways at Beverly. "Did you see if Cliff evacuated?"

She kept her eyes fixed on the horizon. "No idea. Didn't see him after he stopped by my place."

"I did," Dale said. "He was helping people in town board up their windows yesterday."

She felt a confused mix of emotions at that. But then when were her emotions not confused regarding Cliff? It sounded like the Cliff she'd known when he was a boy. How many storms had she seen him help people board up? But it was hard to reconcile that with the man who now wanted to change their hometown into something unrecognizable.

She turned to Dale. "Did you hear anything more about the storm's path?"

"Still tracking northwest. Fort Lauderdale should just get the outer bands, not the worst of it. Better than being on the island, right?" Dale squeezed Maxine's hand.

Beverly looked back at where Magnolia Key had disappeared from view. The wind grew stronger, and more raindrops splattered across the outside deck.

"Should we go down to the cars?" Maxine suggested. "Looks like the weather's starting to turn."

"Probably smart," she agreed. "We've got a long

drive ahead. Might as well stick together in the evacuation traffic."

The three made their way back toward the lower deck, joining the stream of their fellow islanders, all heading into uncertain hours ahead.

CHAPTER 9

Cliff had planned on taking the first ferry out of town, but then he'd driven past Mrs. Henderson's place and saw her still loading things into her car. After he stopped to help her, she actually thanked him and gave him an approving look. Probably the first time she'd ever approved of anything he'd ever done. Then he decided to swing by his mother's house, just to make sure she'd evacuated like she'd said she would.

Cliff pulled up to her house, surprised to see her car still in the driveway. The wind was picking up some, and the palm fronds danced in the breeze. A light rain splattered on his windshield. His mother and Jonah stood on the front porch. He grabbed his raincoat and hurried to the house. As he approached, he heard her calling out Winston's name.

"Mother, what are you still doing here? The last ferry leaves in forty-five minutes."

"Winston got spooked by that branch falling." She pointed to a large palm branch on the ground. "He was standing right beside me one minute, and the next, he bolted away from me. I'm not leaving without him."

"You'll miss the ferry. You need to get out of here."

"I won't leave Winston behind." Her chin lifted in that stubborn way he remembered from his childhood. The way that said arguing would do no good. The same expression she'd worn when he tried to explain why he'd broken curfew or failed algebra.

He had to hand it to her. She was loyal to those she loved. Even if that loyalty was to an aging spaniel. Though he had to admit, he didn't want to leave the old dog behind either. Winston was always happier to see him than his mother was.

"I'll help find him." The words tumbled out before he fully considered how soon the last ferry was leaving and the darkening clouds.

To his surprise, his mother nodded. "Thank you." The appreciation in her eyes made him wonder when he'd last seen that look directed at him.

Jonah stepped forward. "Ellie and I will head up the street. You take the other direction."

"Let me get you a leash." She hurried inside and came back with another leash. "Here, take this."

He took the leash. "Call if you find him. And Mother, we've got thirty minutes max before we need to head to the ferry."

Her lips pressed into a thin line, but she didn't argue. She and Jonah headed up the street, calling Winston's name.

He jogged in the opposite direction, scanning yards and porches for any sign of the dog. He should have thought to grab an umbrella. The rain came down in a steady pour now. The streets were eerily quiet with everyone evacuated. Well, everyone except his mother, Jonah, and him.

"Winston! Here, boy!" He called out as he hurried along the sidewalk. He glanced at his phone and frowned. No cell service. Just great. He finally turned around and headed back, hoping they'd found Winston. Jonah and his mother were just reaching the house but didn't have Winston with them.

"Mother, we have to go right now, or we'll miss the ferry. Winston's a smart dog. He'll find shelter." Unless the storm surge came and Winston couldn't find a safe, high spot, but he wasn't going to say that to his mother.

"I'm not leaving Winston."

"Well, I'm not leaving Ellie here alone."

He looked at both of them and let out a long

sigh. "Let's keep looking. I'll cut over to Bayview. You two try Main." He glanced at his phone again. "Okay, it looks like I have cell service again."

Jonah pulled out his phone. "So do I."

"Service might come and go. Let's meet back here in thirty minutes if the cell service goes out again."

Jonah nodded. "Come on, Ellie."

Her face was etched with worry. Probably not worrying about the approaching storm or the fact they'd missed the last ferry. Worried about Winston.

They headed off to Main Street, then Cliff took First Street over to Bayview. The wind whipped the tree branches, and a lone scrap of paper danced down the street, twisting in the wind.

He kept calling out for Winston but worried his voice was being carried away with the wind. They had to find the dog. He was sure his mother would still be out looking through the actual hurricane if they didn't find Winston first.

He glanced at his watch and realized the last ferry was gone now. Fear crept through him. He hadn't ever planned to sit out another hurricane on this island, but here he was.

He looked down the long street, wondering where to look next. The wind picked up, sending leaves skittering across the pavement. He was at a loss. How long could they wander around calling for Winston?

Suddenly, an idea came to him. His mother would often go over to Bayside B&B to visit with her friend, Darlene, and she often took Winston with her. He turned and cut over to Darlene's B&B and walked around the back to the porch, calling out Winston's name. His heart leapt when he climbed the stairs and spied the dog huddled in the far corner.

He approached slowly. "Hey, buddy. It's okay. Shh… It's okay."

Winston's tail was firmly tucked beneath him with no welcoming wag.

"Hey, Winston. Good to see you. Let's head back home. How about that?" He kept his voice low and calm. When he reached the dog, he carefully hooked the leash on his collar. Relief swept through him.

He snagged his phone and sent out a text. *Found him.*

As he started to lead Winston off the porch, the dog sat down. The dog was having none of it. He reached down and scooped up the dog. "Okay, buddy. You win. I'll carry you."

The dog snuggled against him with a sigh. He climbed down the stairs and hurried back to his mother's house. She was waiting for them as they arrived and rushed out to grab Winston from him. She buried her face in Winston's fur. For a long moment, she remained like that, then she lifted her head. Tears spilled down her cheeks. "Thank you, Cliff. Thank you so much. I just… I can't lose him."

He stared at her for a moment. He'd never seen her cry. Ever. Not when her father died. Not when her husband died. Tears were not something Eleanor Whitmore Griffin ever gave into.

Except now.

The sight of her vulnerability tugged at a place in him he didn't know could still be touched. She had always been a fortress of composure, sure of herself, her emotions carefully guarded behind walls of propriety and pride.

Jonah stepped forward and took her arm, leading her back to the protection of the porch. "Okay, as I see it, we have two choices. We stay here and ride out the storm, or we take my boat and head to the mainland. We won't have all the things you packed up in your car, Ellie."

"I don't care about my things. I have Winston." Her voice cracked.

"I can get us to the mainland, and we'll have to see if we can rent a car to go further inland to safety. It will be a rough ride, but I think that's our best choice."

"I vote taking your boat." Cliff had no desire to stay on the island.

"We could just stay. I'm sure we'll be fine." His mother cuddled the dog closer to her.

"Ellie, we should leave. It's safer."

She finally nodded. "Okay. Let me just grab the bag of Winston's food."

"We'll take my car, Mother. Yours is crammed full of your stuff."

They piled into his car, and when they got to the marina, they followed Jonah to his boat. "Cliff, take Winston for a moment while I help your mother aboard."

By now, he was soaked through and through but hardly cared. He was getting off the island. He wasn't stuck there, sitting out another hurricane. That was all that mattered.

His mother got on board, then Jonah took the dog and climbed on. "Cliff, can you untie us, then climb aboard?"

He did as he was told, then jumped aboard. He joined them in the cabin as the boat sprang to life. Jonah maneuvered it out of the slip and into the bay. The wind had picked up, and the bay was filled with choppy, white-capped waves.

"Cliff, grab the life jackets in that cabinet. I think it wise we put them on." Jonah looked over at his mother. "Ah, it's going to be a rough ride."

He found the life jackets, and they all slipped them on. Jonah's face was etched with concern. "Ellie, why don't you sit down with Winston?"

She settled on a bench with Winston in her arms. She murmured into the dog's ears. "We'll be fine, Winston. We'll get you all safe, you'll see."

Cliff steadied himself by holding onto the polished teak board beneath the window and glanced back at the island as they got further into the bay. The island grew smaller. The sky was the color of an ugly bruise. Rain pounded down on them. And this was just one of the early bands of the storm. The actual hurricane was still a good day and a half out. He wondered what damage it would do. Would the town still be standing?

The boat dipped and plunged again and again, and he was beginning to doubt their choice of trying to get to the mainland. Jonah's face grew tense as they crossed the rough water. He notified the harbor master on the mainland that they were approaching and needed a slip for the boat. The best they could do was tie up at the end of the dock.

As they finally approached the marina, a man in a yellow slicker hurried to the end of the dock. Cliff went out and tossed him a rope, and the man secured the boat.

As they all disembarked, the rain let up, but the wind still whipped around them. Jonah reached for Winston. "I'll carry him. Let's see if we can find a way to get further inland."

"I'm headed across to the other coast if y'all want a ride with me." The man in the slicker held out his hand. "I'm Steve, by the way. Glad you made it safely across the bay. I was just finishing closing the marina when I got your call."

"Thank you, Steve. We'd appreciate the ride out of harm's way." Jonah shook Steve's hand.

Cliff took one last look out at the bay with the angry waves racing across the water. Relief that they'd gotten safely off the island flooded through him, but it didn't stop the anxiety of wondering what they'd come home to.

CHAPTER 10

Beverly leaned against the headboard of her hotel bed, a pillow tucked behind her back, eyes fixed on the television screen. The remote rested in her hand, ready for her constant changing of the channels to see if she could get more information. The same weather map kept appearing with its swirling patterns of red, orange, and yellow moving across the Florida coast.

The forecasters stood in their rain gear, hair whipping in the wind as they gestured dramatically at the storm conditions behind them. One was positioned in Sarasota, ankle-deep in water. Another shouted over the howling winds in Fort Myers. But not a single one was reporting from Magnolia Key.

"They're not even mentioning our island." She frowned at the TV as if that would make news about the island suddenly appear.

Maxine sat at the small round table by the window, scrolling through her phone. "Nothing on social media either. Just general hurricane coverage."

The hotel room was nice, but she longed to be home in her cozy cottage. The room had two queen beds with floral spreads, soothing sage-colored walls, and artwork of the coastline. The air conditioning hummed steadily, keeping tempo with the anxiety thrumming through her.

"I keep thinking about Coastal Coffee. I put up the shutters, moved everything off the floor that I could, but…" She shook her head. "If the storm surge is bad enough…"

"Don't torture yourself." Maxine set her phone down. She crossed the room and sat on the edge of Beverly's bed. "We did everything we could."

"I know. It's just that place is my whole life."

"The building is insured, right?"

She nodded. "But it's not just about the money. It's about…" She struggled to find the right words. "It's everything that place means. All the memories. The community that comes through those doors every day."

The meteorologist on TV was now explaining the hurricane's projected path with unnecessary enthusiasm. She pressed mute, unable to listen to another minute of his animated delivery of potentially devastating news.

"I get it," Maxine said. "But try and remember that whatever happens, you still have that community. The building might change, but the heart of what makes Coastal Coffee special is you."

She gave her friend a grateful smile. "When did you get so wise?"

"Right around the time my life fell apart and I had to put it back together," Maxine said with a wry smile. "Crisis has a way of clarifying what matters."

She reached for her phone on the nightstand, checking it for the tenth time in the last hour. "I wish someone would post something about Magnolia Key. Anything."

"The power's probably out everywhere on the island," Maxine reasoned. "And cell service might be down. And I'm hoping no one stayed, but there are always a handful who refuse to leave."

"You're right. I just hate not knowing."

She unmuted the TV as the weather segment switched to a reporter interviewing evacuees at a shelter a bit inland from Naples. People looked tired and worried, but safe. Children played in the background while adults watched the news on a large-screen TV.

Her phone buzzed, and she grabbed it so quickly she nearly dropped it. "It's Darlene!" She opened the text message.

"What does it say?" Maxine moved closer, peering over her shoulder.

"Made it to my friend's place in Orlando. No news from the island yet. Hope you're safe." She typed a quick reply. "At least she got out okay."

"That's good news. I bet we'll start hearing from more people soon."

She nodded, trying to stay positive. The TV footage now showed waves crashing over a seawall, spraying the surf high up into the air. The ticker at the bottom of the screen reported storm surges of eight to twelve feet in some areas. Her stomach tightened.

"I need some air," she said suddenly, setting the remote down and sliding off the bed. "Want to go down to the lobby for some coffee?"

"Hotel coffee?" Maxine raised an eyebrow. "You'd drink that?"

"Desperate times," she replied with a half-smile.

They took the elevator down to the lobby, which was busier than she expected. Other evacuees milled about, some glued to their phones, others gathered around the large television mounted on the wall which was tuned to the same weather coverage they'd been watching upstairs.

The coffee station in the corner offered self-serve carafes and foam cups. She poured herself a cup and grimaced at the first sip. "Well, that's not Coastal Coffee's brew."

"Told you." Maxine laughed and opted for hot tea instead.

They found seats in a quiet corner, away from the television but with a view of the rain through the large glass doors. The trees outside bent in the wind, though Fort Lauderdale was only getting the outer bands of the storm.

"Remember that hurricane when we were, what? About sixteen?" she asked, staring out at the rain.

"I do."

"The damage was terrible. But we all came together afterward. Everyone helping everyone." She stared down at the coffee cup in her hands. "That's what I love about Magnolia Key. When it counts, people show up for each other."

"You think they will even with all the fighting lately? All the disagreement about Cliff's development?"

She considered that for a moment. "Maybe especially because of that. We might disagree, but it's because everyone cares so deeply about the island." She paused. "I just hope…" She couldn't finish the thought.

"The island will still be there," Maxine said firmly. "It might look different, but it will still be there."

An older couple sat down nearby, the man's phone to his ear as he spoke urgently. "Nothing yet from your brother? Well, keep trying. The news says the barrier islands took a hard hit."

She and Maxine exchanged glances, both thinking the same thing. Magnolia Key was one of those barrier islands.

Dale came walking up to them, interrupting their thoughts. "You'll never guess who I just saw."

"Who?" Maxine patted the seat next to her, and Dale sat down.

"Miss Eleanor, Jonah, and Cliff." Dale laughed. "Oh, and Winston."

"I'm glad they got off the island safely." Maxine leaned against Dale.

"Well, Cliff told quite a story about Winston running off, and while they were trying to find him, the last ferry left."

"Oh, no. How did they get to the mainland?" Beverly asked.

"A very rough ride across the bay on Jonah's boat."

She stood up, and unease flooded through her, as pounding as the storm surge. "I can't just sit here."

"Maybe we should try to get some rest," Maxine suggested. "There's nothing we can do right now except wait."

"I know you're right. But I don't think I'll be able to sleep at all tonight."

"We'll come up to your room, and we'll stay up together." Maxine glanced at Dale, who nodded. "Watch storm coverage and raid the vending machine. At least until you get tired of us and throw us out."

She smiled gratefully at her friend. "I'm glad you're here, Maxine. I don't think I could handle this alone."

"Where else would I be?" Maxine stood and hugged her. "We've weathered worse storms together."

They headed back upstairs, passing more worried-looking evacuees in the lobby. In her room, she turned the TV back on but muted it, watching the images of the storm's aftermath begin to come in from the hardest-hit areas.

The reporter stood in front of a marina where boats had been tossed around like toys. Behind him, a yacht lay on its side, half-submerged in muddy water. The camera panned out to show splintered docks and debris scattered everywhere.

"That's not far from us," she whispered, recognizing the location. "That's only about twenty miles down the coast."

"But twenty miles this way or that makes a huge difference in hurricane damage." Dale sat up straight in his chair, leaning forward. "Turn up the volume. What is he saying? Isn't that the bridge they're building to Magnolia Key?"

She turned on the volume, and the three of them stared at the TV.

"Look at that," she said softly. "That barge took out a huge section of the bridge."

"Well, that's going to change things, isn't it? Doesn't look like we're going to have a bridge connecting the island to the mainland anytime soon." Dale shook his head.

They all stared at the screen and let the news sink in.

She got up and paced the floor, then went over to look out the window. The rain, which had picked up again, dashed against the glass. Somewhere beyond the clouds and the distance was Magnolia Key—her home, her business, her life. And all she could do was wait and hope it would still be there when they returned.

CHAPTER 11

When they finally got the all-clear to return to the island, Beverly headed down to the lobby. She saw Miss Eleanor and Jonah and started to walk over to say hi until she noticed Cliff was with them. She turned away, but obviously not soon enough.

"Beverly." Miss Eleanor waved.

She reluctantly walked across the lobby.

"We need some help. We got a ride over here with a nice young man from the marina, but we need a ride back to the ferry." Miss Eleanor looked at her expectantly. "Do you have room in your car for the three of us?"

The absolute last thing Beverly wanted was to offer a ride to Cliff. Firm no. Just no way.

"I know you're not one of those people who stuff their car full of things. You have your necessary to-go things and a small suitcase when you evacuate, don't you?"

"I, uh… yes. You're right. I don't pack up a lot."

"So, we can get a ride with you back to the ferry?"

Who could ever say no to Miss Eleanor? "Of course." She smiled weakly.

"And Winston, of course."

Winston, she didn't mind. It was Cliff she'd prefer to leave here to his own devices.

"Are you ready to go now? I'm sure the traffic will be horrendous going back across the state, then a long line for the ferry. But I want to get back as soon as possible. We haven't seen too many photos of the island, but the officials have checked it out, and it was safe for residents to return now. Residents only."

"Oh, so Cliff won't be let back on the island?" She had hope.

"No, of course he will. He's my son. They'll let him on."

She had no doubt they would. No one argued with Miss Eleanor.

"I was just getting ready to leave. My car is out front."

Cliff shot her a look, but she couldn't quite read his face. Surprise that she'd said yes? Maybe.

Miss Eleanor, Jonah, and Winston climbed into

her back seat. Which left... only the front seat for Cliff.

He climbed into the front seat, settled in, and fastened his seatbelt. He didn't say a word, which was fine with her. She didn't want to talk to him, anyway.

But the silence stretched out. Uncomfortably so.

She headed back toward the interstate. "I heard the roads are jammed. Lots of people heading back to the Gulf Coast now."

"Yeah." He shifted in his seat and faced forward.

She wished she had Maxine with her, but Maxine was riding with Dale. It would take hours to get back to the ferry. Hours with Cliff sitting next to her. She gripped the steering wheel.

"We're going to be stuck in traffic for hours," she mumbled.

He didn't reply.

The entrance ramp to I-75 was already backed up. Stop. Go. Stop. Go. She crept along, tapping her fingers on the steering wheel.

She glanced over at Cliff, who was staring straight ahead. He had a slight frown on his face, his jaw set.

Miss Eleanor interrupted the silent treatment. "Beverly, I hope Coastal Coffee didn't get too much damage."

She knew what Miss Eleanor was doing. Making

conversation. Trying to get her and Cliff to play nice. "I don't know, Miss Eleanor. I sure hope so."

"A lot of people are going to need coffee once we get back," Jonah said.

Good old Jonah. Playing along.

"We'll get them all fixed up. And I have plenty of coffee beans. I hope." She hadn't really had time to run a full inventory before leaving. And that was if they had electricity or if her generator would work. Or… if there wasn't a lot of damage.

Silence descended again. They inched along. The sun blazed down.

Miss Eleanor tapped Cliff on his shoulder. "And if the island sustained a lot of damage, are you still going ahead with your development?"

"Mother, that's not an appropriate topic of conversation right now."

Oh, here we go. Round number… one hundred? Or however many times the townspeople had argued over the development.

"I just don't think it's appropriate to put that big building there. And at the end of the boardwalk. And the boardwalk that might not even still be there, you know."

Good job, Miss Eleanor. Convince Cliff to abandon the development and then disappear from the island.

She decided to help Miss Eleanor out. "And now that there is all that damage to the bridge they were building, that would impact the build too, wouldn't it? Won't be easy for guests to get to the island. The ferry deters a lot of people.

Cliff gave her a quick look and just shook his head before staring out the windshield again.

They sat in silence again. Minutes ticked past. Maybe hours. They inched along. She took another look at Cliff. He had his elbow on the armrest and his eyes closed. Was he asleep? How could anyone possibly sleep when they didn't know what they would find on the island? There had only been a few photos of it that she could find online.

He opened his eyes, but he still hadn't looked over at her. He really was going to ignore her. Fine. She could just as easily ignore him.

The traffic lightened up just a little, and they got up to maybe forty miles an hour. And then slowed again. Stop. Go. Stop. Go. A familiar pattern now.

"We took my boat from the island to the mainland to evacuate, but we'll take the ferry back to the island today. It will give me time to check out my boat before taking her out again." Jonah broke the silence.

No one answered him.

"This is going to be a long ride home," Jonah tried again.

Miss Eleanor sighed. "How long do you think it will be?"

"Until we get there? Hard to say. But my traffic app shows it's still a mess out there," she answered.

She concentrated on the road. And not on Cliff. How was she supposed to act around him? Ignore him? But they were in confined quarters. It was so awkward. The tension crackled between them.

Cliff surprised her when he finally spoke to her. "Do you want me to drive for a while?"

"No." She gripped the wheel a little harder. She didn't want him driving her car.

"I'm sure you're getting tired. All this stop and go, stop and go."

"I'm fine." She glanced in the rear-view mirror. Miss Eleanor had her eyes closed now.

The traffic picked up a bit. They practically flew down the road... at fifty miles an hour. And then the brake lights ahead came on, and she slowed down again.

As they crept through the Everglades, she counted the minutes until they got across the state and to the ferry landing.

After four full hours, they finally got to the ferry. She joined the long line of cars waiting. There were two ferries running, but it still was going to take a while.

Finally, they reached the front of the line. She drove onto the ferry, parked, and turned off the car. Finally. Longest four hours in the history of time.

"We can get out now." Relief spread through her as she stepped out of the car. She needed to stretch her legs. And walk around.

"I'm going to go upstairs and get some fresh air." And get away from Cliff.

"That's a good idea. Winston, you want to go upstairs?"

They all walked together, an unlikely foursome, toward the stairs leading to the upper deck. Cliff stopped her when they reached the upper deck. "Ah… thanks for the ride."

She just nodded. She spied Maxine just in front of them. "Maxine, wait up."

Maxine turned, and a smile spread across her face.

She hurried to join her friend. They walked across the upper level and slipped away in the crowd. She desperately needed to put some space between herself and Cliff.

They found a spot along the railing. A slight breeze blew, ruffling her hair. She took a deep breath, the salty air filling her lungs. The ferry chugged to life, and its horn blew, signaling its impending departure.

Maxine bumped her hip. "Hey, I saw you in

your car in the line. Couldn't believe my eyes. Cliff was sitting right beside you in your front seat. What's up with that?"

"Let's not talk about it."

Maxine laughed. "Okay, but I admit I was wondering how that all happened."

"Later. We have other things to worry about."

"Sure, we can talk about the weather." Maxine winked. "Can you believe this weather?"

She took in the deep blue sky dotted with fluffy white clouds that drifted lazily across the expanse above them. The sun shone down, warm on her face. It was a perfect beach day. "You'd never know a hurricane swept through here."

"Kind of gives you that false feeling that everything is okay. When you know that the island… Who knows what we'll find?"

"I know." She nodded.

Some of the other passengers had the same idea, joining them on the top deck. Everyone stared out at the water, quiet and lost in their own thoughts. Anxious to get back and see what they would find.

She focused on a bird gliding effortlessly across the water. Then it dove down and came back up with something in its beak. Nature went on. No matter what. Storms might come and go, but life continued.

And it would for them, too. They'd rebuild.

Whatever that looked like. She'd get the coffee shop up and running. That was her main priority at the moment.

The ferry started moving, and she gripped the railing. They headed out into the bay and soon passed the wreckage of much of what had been the new bridge. A large barge was lodged against it. A couple of sections had completely disappeared, and more looked damaged.

Murmurs swept across the deck.

"Wow, it's all just gone."

"Bet that will set things back a while."

"Might never get rebuilt."

She spotted Cliff on the other side of the ferry. He was staring at what was left of the bridge, probably wondering what that would do to his project.

With any luck, it would shut him down.

She pushed all thoughts of Cliff away as they got closer to the island. She let out a deep breath as the island came into view.

Maxine squeezed her hand. "There it is."

She could make out some of the buildings as they got closer. From their view, it didn't appear too bad. But she knew looks could be deceiving.

They got closer. Closer. It looked like some of the palm trees had been denuded of their fronds.

"Looks like Darlene's B&B is still standing." She pointed.

Maxine broke into a smile. "And not too much damage from what I can see, but you never know."

"Hard to tell until we get over there.

The ferry slowed, getting ready to dock. The closer they got, the clearer it became that the island had sustained some major hits. Downed trees were scattered about. A few large boats were tilted onto the dock of the marina, half-submerged in the water.

They got closer still. People pointed. And whispered. And gasped. She held her breath.

The captain made an announcement. "We're pulling into the dock now. Please return to your vehicles."

Everyone started edging their way toward the stairs, antsy to get off now. A few more minutes. And then she'd know.

She and Maxine headed downstairs. They found Dale by his car. "I'm going to head straight to Second Finds and check out the damage."

Maxine nodded. "I'm going with Beverly to check out Coastal Coffee."

She looked at Maxine gratefully.

Dale gave Maxine a quick kiss. "I'll come by and check on you two soon."

They got into her car. One by one, the cars were directed off the ferry, which seemed like an agonizingly slow process today.

Just when she didn't think she could wait a

second longer, it was their turn, and she followed the car ahead of her down the ramp and onto the island.

She was home. On her beloved island. Now to see what damage had been done.

CHAPTER 12

Cliff guided his mother and Jonah toward his car in the ferry parking lot. A few cars had their windshields broken, but luckily his was intact. His mother's sharp intake of breath at the sight of fallen trees, broken glass, and scattered debris across the area made him reach for her elbow.

"Mother, let me help you."

She pulled away. "I can manage." But she gripped Jonah's arm instead.

He opened the passenger door for her, but she slid into the back seat with Jonah.

"The wind damage looks extensive," Jonah said as they drove past broken shop windows—the unlucky ones whose hurricane shutters or boards hadn't stayed in place. A random table rested on its side on the sidewalk. Shop owners were busy taking down shutters to assess the damage.

"We might have some trouble getting through." He slowly inched the car along, dodging items in the street. "We'll have to go the long way around." He pointed to a large tree that blocked their path. "This road is impassable."

They circled around several other streets, each one exhibiting some degree of destruction. It was like entering a maze. Right, left, right, then a dead end. Backtrack, then left, right, and circle back to the left. They ended up on Jonah's street.

"Want to stop and check your house?"

"Ellie, is that okay? I know you're anxious to check yours."

"That's silly. We're here. Go run in and see how it fared."

She tapped her fingers on the armrest while Jonah disappeared into his house.

He was back within a few minutes. "I'm good. Looks like no damage inside. A tree down in the back. And someone's lost rocking chair is smack in the middle of the yard, acting like it belongs there." He slid back into the car. "Let's go check on Ellie's house."

He finally pulled onto Seaside Avenue and neared his mother's home.

"Oh, no." Her gasp made him slam on the brakes.

The massive live oak that had graced his mother's front yard for over a century had toppled onto the wraparound porch, crushing the entire east end. Broken roof tiles created a terra cotta pathway across the lawn.

He parked and hurried around to help his mother from the car, but she was already out and walking toward the house. She stopped at the edge of the yard, her hand pressed to her chest.

"That tree survived every hurricane since before I was born." Her voice wavered slightly. "Lost a huge section years ago, but it's still been standing."

"We'll get it cleared away," Jonah reassured her. "I'll make some calls."

"My mother used to sit under that tree and read to me when I was a little girl."

She headed toward the porch, and Jonah took her elbow. "Careful there, Ellie." They picked their way across the lawn, avoiding the broken tiles and smaller branches.

The end of the porch roof was gone. Splintered wood lay scattered across the yard, mingling with broken roof tiles. Chunks of the porch railing were gone. Pieces of it jutted out at odd angles.

They walked carefully up the steps, gingerly at first. He wasn't sure if the whole porch might give way with too much weight. A large chunk of the roofline had collapsed near the front window, taking out some decorative corbels and a whole section of guttering. He could glimpse a section of exposed roofing.

"Got your key, Ellie?"

She nodded, her attention on the mess of her once-immaculate yard.

Jonah took the key from her outstretched hand and inserted it into the lock. He turned the knob, and they stepped inside. The interior seemed relatively untouched at first.

"I want to look upstairs." She hurried toward the long staircase that led to the second floor.

He and Jonah followed her up the steps. He glanced up the hallway ceiling. There was no sign of damage there, and the new impact window had held at the end of the hallway.

"Oh, no." She stood in the doorway of the master bedroom.

He walked up to her and peered inside. Water stains bloomed across the ceiling. A section of the plaster hung down. It seemed the roof damage was worse than he'd anticipated. Water dripped onto the carpet, making a squishing sound when he walked on it.

"Looks like we'll need to get someone out here to fix the roof," he said, trying to maintain a neutral tone. No use saying I told you so about the dangers of staying put during a hurricane.

"I'll take a look around the rest of the upstairs." He moved down the hallway, checking each room. One of the guest rooms had leaked around the window, and rain had soaked the curtains and pooled on the wooden floor. A section of the ceiling had water stains.

His mother came and stood in the doorway, shaking her head. Jonah appeared beside her. "Lots of repairs needed, Ellie."

"Well, we'll get someone started on them right away."

They headed back toward his mother's room, and he surveyed the water-damaged ceiling, calculating the extent of repairs needed. One section looked ready to collapse entirely, and he didn't like the idea of her staying beneath it.

"This is worse than I thought," he muttered, running his fingers along a crack in the plaster. Water had seeped in along the entire eastern side of the house where the tree had crashed through part of the roof structure.

His mother stood in the doorway, her shoulders slumped slightly as she surveyed the damage to her home. He couldn't remember the last time he'd seen her look so… defeated.

"I'll call someone to tarp the roof right away." He pulled out his phone. "Shouldn't be too difficult to get a crew out here quickly."

Jonah stepped forward, placing a hand on her shoulder. "Ellie, you can't stay here. Not with all this damage."

She straightened her spine. "Of course I can stay here. This is my home."

"The ceiling could come down at any moment," Jonah insisted, gesturing to the sagging plaster. "And the house isn't weathertight anymore. If it rains again—"

"I've lived through worse."

Cliff exchanged a glance with Jonah. His mother's stubbornness was legendary. Once she made a decision, changing her mind was impossible.

"Mother, Jonah's right." He surprised himself by agreeing with Jonah. "It's not safe here."

She scoffed. "I'll have a tarp put up and sleep downstairs."

Jonah shook his head firmly. "Ellie, be reasonable. You should stay with me. My place didn't take any damage."

"That wouldn't be proper, Jonah. What would people say?" She tucked back a lock of hair, avoiding Jonah's gaze.

Cliff almost laughed. His mother, worried about appearances at a time like this? The town was half-destroyed by a hurricane, and she was concerned about gossip.

"Mother, I think propriety is the least of anyone's concerns right now. The whole town just survived a hurricane. No one's going to be talking about where you're sleeping."

"Nevertheless," she insisted. "It isn't proper."

Jonah sighed. "Ellie, please. It just makes sense.

My place has three bedrooms. You'd have your own space."

"I agree with Jonah," he insisted, surprising himself again. "You should stay at his place until we can get repairs done here."

She looked back and forth between the two men, clearly outnumbered. "Fine," she relented, though her tone suggested she wasn't happy about it. "But just until things are cleaned up and enough repairs are made for me to move back."

Jonah nodded, relief evident on his face. "Of course. Just until then."

"Now, you two take Winston downstairs. Find more of his food, and grab his bed from the front room. I'll need to pack some things."

They headed downstairs, and once she was out of earshot, Jonah turned to him. "Thanks for backing me up. She listens to you more than she lets on."

He raised an eyebrow, doubtful. "Does she? That's news to me."

"She does," Jonah insisted. "Even when she disagrees with you."

He wasn't convinced, but he appreciated the sentiment. He moved to head to the kitchen to find Winston's food, but Jonah placed a hand on his arm, stopping him.

"Cliff, why don't you stay with us too?"

The question caught him off guard. "What?"

"Stay with us," Jonah repeated. "At my place. It's big enough for the three of us."

Cliff stared at him, trying to read his intentions. "I don't think that's necessary. I can find somewhere else to stay."

"Where? There's so much damage, and most rentals will be booked with people displaced by the storm."

He had a point. Cliff hadn't thought that far ahead. He'd planned to check on his mother and then figure out his own accommodations.

"I appreciate the offer," Cliff said carefully, "but my mother and I under the same roof? That doesn't usually end well."

Jonah chuckled. "I've noticed. But it's temporary, and I think Ellie would feel better knowing you're safe too."

He doubted that. His relationship with his mother had always been complicated. She'd never approved of his choices, his career, or much of anything else about him. The development project had only widened the existing gap between them.

"I'm not sure that's true," he said.

"Trust me," Jonah replied. "She worries about you more than she lets on."

He considered the offer. Staying with his mother and Jonah would be uncomfortable, but it would also give him a chance to assess the damage to her house, and he could coordinate repairs more easily if he was nearby. Despite what his mother may think, he did care about the family home. And Jonah was right—finding other accommodations would be difficult with the storm damage.

"All right," he said finally. "But just until I can make other arrangements."

Jonah smiled, clapping him on the shoulder. "Good. I'll find Winston's bed, you find his food, then let's go see if Ellie needs any help."

They found her in her bedroom, carefully folding clothes into a small suitcase. She looked up when they entered.

"Jonah has invited me to stay at his place too." He couldn't help noticing the tentative sound in his voice.

She paused in her packing. "Both of us?"

"Yes," Jonah confirmed. "It makes sense. We'll all be more comfortable there than trying to find other arrangements with the island in this state."

She resumed her packing, not making eye contact. "I suppose that's sensible."

Coming from his mother, that was practically enthusiastic approval. He shared a look with Jonah, who seemed pleased by the development.

She finished packing, carefully placing her toiletries in a small travel case. As they prepared to leave, she stopped in the doorway, looking back at her bedroom. "This house has stood for over a hundred years. It's survived every storm that's come its way."

"And it will survive this one too," he assured her. "I'll make sure of it."

She gave him a look he couldn't quite interpret —surprise mixed with something else. Not quite gratitude, but close.

"See that you do," she said, but the usual bite was missing from her words.

They made their way downstairs, and Winston trotted behind them, seemingly unbothered by the chaos.

His mother stood in the foyer, looking around at her home. For a moment, he caught a glimpse of vulnerability in her expression—something he rarely saw. Then she straightened her shoulders, and the moment passed.

"Let's not dawdle," she said briskly. "There's much to be done."

As they left the house, he caught Jonah's eye. The man gave him a small nod of acknowledgment.

He was going to be living in the same house as his mother again after all these years. Something he'd never thought would happen.

Beverly stood in front of Coastal Coffee, her heart sinking as she took in the damage. Broken roof tiles littered the sidewalk, some cracked into jagged pieces while others remained mostly intact. At least they'd been spared the storm surge that had devastated communities to the south.

"It's not as bad as I feared." She tried to sound optimistic for Maxine's sake. "Roof damage, but the building looks solid."

Maxine squeezed her shoulder. "We can handle some missing tiles. That's fixable."

She nodded, pulling the keys from her pocket. Her hand trembled slightly as she approached the hurricane shutters covering the front door. Years of running this place, weathering economic downturns, seasonal fluctuations, other hurricanes, and now this. She swallowed hard, trying to prepare herself for what she might find inside.

"Ready?" Maxine asked, positioning herself beside Beverly.

"As ready as I'll ever be." She unlatched the hurricane shutters and pulled them open. The metal groaned in protest after being battered by wind and rain. She slid the key into the lock on the door, holding her breath as she pushed open the door and stepped inside.

The darkness enveloped them immediately. Without electricity, the cafe felt eerily quiet and unfamiliar.

"I can't see a thing." She fished her phone from her pocket and turned on the flashlight. Maxine did the same, and they swept their beams around the room.

The light revealed tables and chairs still neatly arranged where they'd left them before the evacuation. At least that was good. Her beam caught movement, and she startled before realizing it was just their reflection in the large mirror behind the counter.

"Let's get some more light in here." Her voice echoed slightly in the space. "Help me with these other shutters."

They stepped back outside and worked methodically, removing the hurricane shutters from the front windows. Then they took down the shutters covering the kitchen windows. Each one they took down allowed more natural daylight to filter into the cafe, gradually illuminating the interior.

When they'd removed enough shutters to see properly, they stepped back inside. The floor near one side of the cafe glistened with water.

"Looks like we got some water coming in." She pointed toward the small puddles forming near some tables near the back.

"Probably from those missing roof tiles." Maxine followed behind her. "Let's check the kitchen."

She pushed open the swinging door to the kitchen, bracing herself. The room appeared largely untouched, though water had seeped through the ceiling in spots, leaving small puddles on the stainless steel counters and floor.

"Could be worse." She opened the refrigerator to check its contents. "We'll need to toss most of this."

"The structure seems intact. No major damage that I can see."

She moved to the storage closet and pulled out the mop and bucket. "Let's clean up this water before it causes more problems."

As they worked side by side, mopping up the puddles, a strange mix of emotions filled her. Relief that her beloved cafe hadn't been destroyed, gratitude for Maxine's steady presence, and yet a lingering anxiety about what would come next.

"I wonder how long we'll be without power," she said, wringing the mop into the bucket. "The generator can keep the refrigerator running, and run the coffee makers, but we can't open without electricity."

"They usually prioritize getting power back to the businesses on Main Street." Maxine shrugged. "Maybe a day or two if we're lucky? We could do a limited menu—cold sandwiches, things that don't need heating."

She nodded, considering the idea. "If I can get supplies brought over here, that would work. People will need somewhere to gather, to talk about the storm and check on each other."

They finished mopping and moved to inspect the rest of the cafe more thoroughly. She climbed carefully onto a chair to examine the ceiling where water had come through.

"We'll need tarps until we can get the roof fixed," she said, stepping down. "And I'll run the dehumidifier once the power's back on to prevent mold."

"I'm adding that to the list," Maxine said, already jotting notes on her phone. "What else?"

She looked around at her cafe—still standing, still whole in all the ways that mattered most. The water damage was manageable. The broken tiles outside could be replaced. The food that spoiled was just inventory, not the heart of what made Coastal Coffee special.

"We need to check the generator in the storage shed," she said, moving toward the back door. "And make sure the coffee machines weren't damaged by any water."

They stepped into the small area beside the cafe where she had a small storage shed. The door hung slightly ajar, apparently blown open during the storm. Inside, the generator stood untouched.

"Looks okay," she said, checking the fuel level. "We can run it in shifts to keep the refrigeration going until the power's back."

As they made their way back inside, she paused at the pastry counter. The glass display case remained intact, though empty. She'd cleared it before evacuating.

"Remember when we used to pretend to run a cafe when we were kids?" she turned and asked Maxine suddenly. "You'd take orders, and I'd make coffee out of mud and water." Her lips curved up in a smile at the memory.

Maxine laughed. "And we'd serve leaves as cookies to all our stuffed animals."

"Look at us now." She gestured around. "Still playing cafe, just with real food and actual customers."

"And a hurricane thrown in for excitement." Maxine grinned.

Some of the tension began to ease from her shoulders. The tension that had been riding there since they first heard about the approaching storm. "Yes, we'll be okay."

They continued their assessment, checking pipes for leaks and surveying every corner of the cafe. Maxine made more notes of supplies they'd need—tarps, roofing materials, cleaning product. Beverly photographed the damage for insurance purposes.

"So, what do you think? Can we open tomorrow, even with limited service?" Maxine asked after they'd finished their inspection.

She looked around at her cafe, mentally calculating what needed to be done. "If we get the generator running to make coffee, maybe the day after tomorrow. People will need coffee and something normal after all this."

"And a place to share their storm stories."

Beverly nodded. "That's what Coastal Coffee has always been about—not just the food and drinks, but the community. The connections."

She walked to the front windows, now uncovered and letting in streams of late afternoon sunlight. Outside, she could see others returning to their businesses, assessing damage, and already starting repairs. Magnolia Key was wounded but standing.

"First thing tomorrow, we'll get those tarps," she decided. "See if we can get someone to put them up on the roof. Then clean everything from top to bottom. If the power's still out, we'll get the generator working."

Maxine came to stand beside her at the window. "One step at a time."

She turned to look at her cafe again, seeing it not as it was now—slightly damaged and dark—but as it would be again soon, full of light and conversation, the heart of her community. Her home.

"One step at a time," she agreed.

CHAPTER 14

Beverly wiped down the coffee counter for the third time that morning, finding comfort in the familiar motion. Two days after the hurricane, she'd managed to get Coastal Coffee open. Not at full capacity, but enough to provide a gathering spot for the community. The generator hummed steadily, powering the coffee machines, the refrigerator, and a few essential lights.

She'd found a handyman to secure tarps over the damaged section of the roof and spent all day yesterday cleaning up the interior. Thankfully, her own cottage had sustained only minor damage. She'd found a few downed tree branches and some garden destruction, but nothing structural. She counted herself among the fortunate ones.

The morning crowd had been steady since she

opened. When Nash Carlisle had popped in first thing as usual, congratulating her on opening, it made her feel like life was returning to normal. People wandered in with weary smiles, grateful for a semblance of normal amid the chaos of recovery. Without electricity across most of the island, her generator-powered coffee had become something of a luxury.

"Morning, Miss Beverly." Tim Marshall walked through the open door. "Rumor has it that you have hot coffee and some baked goods."

"I do." She smiled, gesturing to the pastry case where she'd arranged the goods Julie had sent over from The Sweet Shoppe at Lighthouse Point. "Belle Island barely got touched by the storm, so Julie's been baking up a storm for us—no pun intended."

Tim chuckled as he approached the counter. "That's really something, isn't it? Just a few miles can make all the difference between getting flattened and barely getting rained on."

"That's hurricanes for you." She poured him a cup of coffee and placed a muffin on a plate. "How's your place holding up?"

"Lost a few shingles. Nothing I can't fix." He took the coffee gratefully. "My wife is staying with our daughter in St. Pete's until the power comes back. Me, I'd rather be here helping where I can."

She nodded, understanding completely. She'd

rather be here too, doing what she could to help restore Magnolia Key.

"More coffee, Mrs. Henderson?" Beverly asked, approaching a table where the woman sat enjoying her first cup.

"Please, dear," Mrs. Henderson replied, holding up her mug. "I can't tell you how good it feels to sit somewhere that isn't that stuffy evacuation center."

She waited on more customers, slowly making her way to the front of the cafe, and glanced out the front window, surveying Main Street. Workers from the electric company had arrived that morning, and their trucks lined the street as they worked to restore power. Some storefronts remained boarded up while others showed signs of activity as owners returned to assess and repair.

Her gaze stopped abruptly when she spotted a familiar figure on a ladder propped against Patty Miller's gift shop. Cliff Griffin balanced on the roof, hammering down a blue tarp while Patty stood below, looking up anxiously.

She stared, surprised to see him helping. She hadn't expected Cliff to stick around after the storm, let alone pitch in with repairs. He wore a T-shirt darkened with sweat, his movements efficient as he secured the tarp over Patty's damaged roof.

Mrs. Henderson came up beside her and glanced out the window. "Is that Cliff out there?

You know, before the storm hit, he helped me out too. He was a troublemaker in school, that's for sure, but he's done some nice, helpful things along the way. I think he really believes this project of his will help the town."

"Maybe." She wasn't really willing to give Cliff credit for that.

Mrs. Henderson left, and Beverly watched as Cliff climbed down from the ladder, exchanged words with Patty, and then began folding the ladder. Even from this distance, she could see Patty's grateful expression as she reached out to touch Cliff's arm in thanks.

The man did surprise her sometimes. Then she reminded herself that he'd surprised her all those years ago when they were going to leave the island together but instead he'd left her without a word. Yes, he was always full of surprises.

She shook her head, chasing away the memories, and moved back behind the counter, pleased to see the cafe filling up with familiar faces. People continued to stop by for coffee and a bit of news.

And the chatter was filled with Cliff.

Cliff fixing Mr. Peterson's porch steps.

Cliff helping clear debris from the library's yard.

Cliff delivering cases of water to the senior center.

Who was this Cliff Griffin everyone was

chattering about? Not the Cliff she knew. Had everyone forgotten about his development and how it would change the town?

She continued to wait on customers, relishing the familiar routine. She looked up and saw Darlene come in. "Heard you were open." Darlene hugged her. "I'm so glad you didn't have more damage."

Maxine came over. "Why don't you sit down with Darlene for a bit? You haven't stopped since we opened this morning."

"Thanks, that sounds wonderful." She looked at her friend gratefully and grabbed a couple of cups of coffee.

"How's the B&B, Darlene?" she asked as she sat down and slid a cup over to Darlene.

"Could be worse. Some water damage in two rooms on the bay side. The insurance adjuster's coming tomorrow. My gardens are in ruins. Still a lot of cleanup to do. The B&B is filled with residents whose homes sustained a lot of damage. I'm glad to have a place for them to stay."

"Let me know if you need any help. Maxine and I could come by after we close up here," she offered.

"Thanks, but I think I have it covered. Say, did you see the bridge when you came back to the island? Quite a sight, wasn't it?"

"I heard it might be months until they can safely get the barge moved. Then they'll assess the damage. I've heard talk that there isn't the funding to replace it, and the project might get cancelled for now."

Darlene shook her head. "I have to admit, that wouldn't bother me much. It was just going to bring more traffic to town. Change everything. I like Magnolia Key just like it is."

They sat and chatted, but thankfully, not one word about Cliff. Darlene left after a bit, and Beverly joined Maxine at the counter. "Thanks for giving me a little break."

"No problem."

"I saw Cliff helping Patty with her roof," Maxine said casually, glancing sideways at her. "He's been all over town the past two days, from what I've heard."

She busied herself arranging napkins. "So I've heard."

"Interesting, isn't it?" Maxine pressed. "The man who wants to change Magnolia Key with his high-rise is now helping folks repair what they already have."

"People are complicated," she replied, not wanting to admit that seeing Cliff help had stirred conflicting emotions within her. "Maybe he feels guilty about pushing his development before the storm hit."

"Maybe." Maxine didn't sound convinced. "Or maybe there's more to him than we've been willing to see."

She turned away from her friend's knowing gaze and began wiping down an already clean table. "Either way, it's good he's helping. The town needs all hands right now."

A new group of customers entered, saving her from further conversation about Cliff. She greeted them warmly, taking their orders and moving efficiently behind the counter.

For the next hour, she kept herself busy, refilling coffee cups, making more sandwiches when supplies ran low, and listening to stories of storm damage and narrow escapes. All the while, she found her gaze drifting to the window, watching as Cliff finished with Patty's roof and moved on to help Jake at the hardware store unload a truck that had just arrived with supplies.

Against her will, memories surfaced—younger versions of themselves, Cliff always ready to lend a hand when someone needed it. Before he'd left her waiting at the ferry. Before he'd become the developer who wanted to change their island with tall buildings and tourist attractions.

"Would you look at that?" Rachel Masters came up beside her and nodded toward the window. "Never thought I'd see the day when Cliff Griffin would be up fixing Patty's roof. Or helping unload a truck."

She nodded, not sure how to answer that.

"People can surprise you, I suppose." Rachel shrugged before heading outside.

"Penny for your thoughts," a voice said from behind her, startling her from her reverie. Miss Eleanor stood there, impeccably dressed despite the circumstances, with Winston on his leash beside her.

"Just wondering when the power might come back on," she lied, turning to Miss Eleanor with a smile. "Can I get you some coffee? I don't have your cream for it, though. Didn't come in with the supplies. Or I have some sweet tea."

"Tea would be lovely." Miss Eleanor took a seat at her usual table, and Beverly returned with the tea. "Jonah's helping with the cleanup at the church, and I thought I'd take Winston for his walk. The poor creature's been quite disturbed by the whole ordeal."

"How's your house coming along?" Of course, everyone in town knew Miss Eleanor's house had been damaged.

Miss Eleanor sighed, stroking Winston's head as he settled at her feet. "It's a disaster, frankly. The contractor says it could be weeks before the repairs are complete."

She noticed Miss Eleanor didn't admit she was staying at Jonah's house, but everyone in town knew that fact too. And surprisingly, Cliff was also staying there.

Miss Eleanor took a sip of her tea. "I saw Cliff

helping Jake unload a truck of supplies on my walk over. He seems determined to make himself useful."

"Yes, he's been busy," she answered noncommittally.

"He always did have a good heart, beneath all that stubbornness," Miss Eleanor remarked, surprising Beverly with the almost complimentary assessment of her son.

Not knowing how to respond, she simply nodded and excused herself to help other customers. The cafe had grown busy again with the lunch crowd—if a person could call cold sandwiches and pastries lunch. Still, no one complained. They were just grateful to have somewhere to gather.

As she worked, her thoughts returned to Cliff and his unexpected helpfulness after the storm. It didn't align with her image of the man who'd proposed a development that would forever change Magnolia Key's skyline. The man who'd abandoned her years ago without a word.

She'd told Maxine that people are complicated, and now she found herself considering the truth of those words. Could Cliff be both the developer determined to build his high-rise and the man currently helping his neighbors without being asked? Could he be both the boy who'd broken her heart and the man who remembered how to be part of this community when it needed him most?

She wasn't ready to forgive him. Not for the past, and not for his present plans for the island. But as she watched him through the window, helping and sweating alongside everyone else, she had to admit there might be more to Cliff Griffin than she'd allowed herself to see.

Beverly had gotten Coastal Coffee back up and running, but a week after returning, she was still facing challenges. At least the electricity was back on. That was a blessing. But the roof leak had gotten worse because the tarp covering it came loose in a storm a few days ago. Every time it rained—which seemed to be daily lately—she had to place buckets strategically around the cafe.

"I swear the insurance company is trying to wait me out," she said to Maxine, who was sitting at the counter nursing her second cup of coffee after the morning rush. "They came out to assess the damage, but then crickets. Nothing about the amount they'll pay toward the claim."

Her friend nodded sympathetically. "I get it. Dale's dealing with the same thing at Second Finds.

The adjusters are swamped with claims all over the island."

She sighed, swiping a cloth across the counter. "That's just part of it. I've called every contractor on my list, and they're all booked solid for the next month. At this rate, I'll be serving coffee with umbrellas inside the shop by next week."

"That could be a catchy new theme," Maxine quipped. "Coastal Coffee: Where It Rains Indoors!"

Despite her frustration, she smiled. "Very funny. I just need to get it fixed before the next big storm hits. If the roof doesn't get repaired soon, I'll have to have the tarp redone."

She glanced out the window, her attention caught by a red pickup truck that slowed as it passed Coastal Coffee. Was that Cliff driving a truck? Her stomach did an unwelcome flip.

"Speaking of repairs," Maxine said, following her gaze, "isn't that Cliff in that truck? I heard he's been helping out all over town."

She pressed her lips together. "Yes. Unfortunately, I was raised too well to dislike anyone completely. He's been fixing roofs, clearing debris, and even helped Tori get her generator running." She shook her head slightly. "It's… confusing."

"What has ever *not* been confusing between you and Cliff?"

"I know, I know." She paused and shrugged.

"He's the same man who wants to build that monstrosity on the boardwalk, but then he turns around and helps neighbors fix their hurricane damage. I don't know how to reconcile those two sides of the man."

The bell over the door jingled, and she looked up to see the very subject of their conversation walk in. Cliff wore a simple gray T-shirt with work pants, and his hands showed evidence of manual labor. He hesitated just inside the door, as if uncertain of his welcome.

She felt several emotions wash through her at once—annoyance, confusion, and *something else*. After all she'd seen him do for the town over the past week, she couldn't just throw him out, no matter how much a part of her wanted to.

"Take a seat anywhere," she said, gesturing to the empty tables.

He looked genuinely surprised, his eyebrows rising slightly before he nodded. But instead of sitting at a table, he walked over and took a seat at the counter, a couple of stools away from Maxine.

"Morning, Maxine," he said with a polite nod.

"Cliff." Maxine gave Beverly a meaningful look before picking up her coffee mug. "I should get going. Dale needs help inventorying what survived the storm at the shop." She slid off her stool and leaned closer to her. "Call me later."

Beverly turned to Cliff, who sat quietly waiting.

"What can I get you?" she asked, keeping her tone professional.

"Just coffee. And maybe one of those blueberry muffins, if you have any left."

She nodded, pouring him a cup and placing a muffin on a plate. Setting both in front of him, she noticed the bandage wrapped around his left hand.

"What happened there?" she asked before she could stop herself.

He glanced at his hand. "Cut myself helping replace some siding at the library yesterday. Nothing serious."

She nodded, then found herself saying, "I've heard you've been helping out all over town."

He shrugged, taking a sip of his coffee. "Seems like the right thing to do. I've got the skills, and there's plenty of work to go around."

"And where's your Mercedes? I saw you driving a truck this morning." It appeared she was full of questions for Cliff Griffin today.

"Sold it over on the mainland. A truck makes more sense for now. I've been hauling things. Supplies, lumber, roofing material. Can't do that with a Mercedes, now can I?"

"No, I guess not." His practical decision surprised her.

Through the window behind him, she could see the blue tarp covering a section of her roof, flapping slightly in the morning breeze. She bit her lip, pride and practicality warring within her.

"How's your place?" he asked as he turned to follow her gaze. "I noticed the tarp when I drove by."

"It's seen better days," she admitted reluctantly.

He nodded, breaking off a piece of his muffin. "Finding someone to do repairs must be challenging right now."

"That's putting it mildly." She laughed dryly. "I've called everyone I know. They're all booked solid for weeks. I should have called the very first thing after arriving back here on the island. I know better."

He was quiet for a moment, chewing thoughtfully. "I could take a look if you want. No strings attached," he added quickly. "Just a neighbor helping a neighbor."

She studied him, searching for any hidden motives. "Why would you do that?" She'd hardly said a civil word to the man since his return to the island and his ridiculous project at the end of the boardwalk.

He met her gaze directly. "Because Coastal Coffee is important to this town. And because…" He hesitated. "Because I know I'm not exactly your favorite person right now."

That was an understatement, but she couldn't deny she needed help.

"I don't need charity," she said finally.

"It's not charity. It's… making amends, maybe." He took another sip of his coffee. "Or just being a decent human being during a crisis. Take your pick."

Despite herself, Beverly felt a smile tugging at the corner of her mouth. "When did you learn to fix roofs, anyway?"

"I… uh, after I, uh… left… I worked some construction. And I've done plenty of hands-on work with my developments over the years. Contrary to what some might think, I don't just sit in an office pushing paperwork."

She considered him for a long moment. The pragmatic side of her brain was screaming to accept his help. She truly had no other immediate options. The emotional side was throwing up caution flags.

"No strings attached?" she confirmed.

"None whatsoever," he promised. "I'll fix your roof, and then you can go back to being justifiably annoyed with me about my development plans."

That drew a reluctant laugh from her. "I suppose I can't argue with that logic." She gestured to the ceiling, where a water stain was spreading. "When could you look at it? I do have some leftover tiles from the last time I had the roof repaired. Not sure if I have enough for all the damage, though."

"I can come back this afternoon after I finish at

Mrs. Henderson's place," he offered. "I'm helping her replace some broken windows."

She nodded, still not entirely comfortable but too practical to refuse.

"I'll be here at three," he said as he finished his coffee.

He stood up, pulling out his wallet, but she waved him off. "It's on the house. Consider it a down payment on roof repairs."

His lips curved into a genuine smile that, much to her dismay, reminded her of the boy she'd known years ago. "Deal." He headed for the door, then turned back. "Beverly?"

"Yes?"

"Thank you. For not throwing me out on sight." He sent her a lazy grin.

Before she could respond, he was gone, leaving her with a kaleidoscope of splintering emotions. She watched him climb into his truck and drive away, wondering if she'd just made a terrible mistake or a levelheaded decision.

The logical part of her insisted it was just about getting her roof fixed. But something deeper whispered that by letting Cliff help, she was opening a door she'd kept firmly closed for decades.

CHAPTER 16

Eleanor sat in Jonah's living room, staring at the ceiling fan as it made lazy circles above her head. Winston was curled at her feet, occasionally twitching in his sleep. The window was slightly open, allowing the breeze to carry in the sounds of hammering and distant voices as people worked to rebuild their homes.

"More tea?" Jonah asked, holding up the pot.

"No, thank you. I've had enough." She glanced at the clock on the mantel. Cliff had left hours ago, after saying something about helping Mrs. Henderson with her damaged fence. His newfound helpfulness bewildered her.

Jonah settled into the armchair across from her. "You know, I saw Cliff at the library helping board up those broken windows, and a few days ago, he was helping Jake unload some more supplies for the hardware store."

Her fingers found their way to the arm of the sofa, tapping rhythmically. "Yes, well, I suspect he has ulterior motives. Get everyone to like him so they'll support that high-rise he wants to build."

"Maybe." Jonah shrugged. "Or maybe he's just helping because help is needed."

"Cliff doesn't do things without getting something in return. That's not how he operates."

"People can change, Ellie."

She shot him a look. "At his age? Unlikely."

"You changed." Jonah smiled mischievously. "You weren't always the warm, cuddly woman you are today."

Despite herself, her lips twitched upward. "Careful there, sir."

He was still grinning as he reached for his cup. "I'm just saying, people can surprise you. Even your son."

She sighed. The last few weeks had left her feeling adrift. Her home damaged, her town in disarray, and now her son acting completely out of character. Nothing made sense anymore.

"Anyway, it seems like he's helping half the town," she admitted reluctantly. "Darlene mentioned he brought over generators from the mainland to the senior center when their power went out."

"He's been busy," Jonah agreed.

"But why? Why now? He hasn't cared about this town in years. He left suddenly years ago and barely came back to visit. And when he did return, it was to build some enormous eyesore that would ruin everything that makes Magnolia Key special."

"Maybe the hurricane changed his perspective."

"A hurricane doesn't change who someone is at their core." But even as she said the words, doubt crept in. She'd seen the look on Cliff's face when they'd returned to find her house damaged. Real concern, not the polished sympathy he usually displayed.

"I just don't understand him," she admitted.

"Have you tried asking him why he's helping?"

"No." She folded her arms across her chest.

Jonah chuckled. "You two are so alike sometimes."

"We are nothing alike," she protested.

"Stubborn. Proud. Unwilling to admit when you might be wrong." He counted off on his fingers. "Should I continue?"

"You've said more than enough."

He smiled, unaffected by her warning tone. "You know what I think? I think he's trying to make amends in his own way."

"By fixing roofs and clearing debris? That doesn't erase years of absence. Or his plans to destroy the character of this town."

"Maybe not. But it's something." He paused. "You know, yesterday I overheard him talking to the mayor about establishing a fund for residents who didn't have adequate insurance."

That caught her by surprise. "A fund? With whose money?"

"His, apparently. And maybe a fundraiser."

That didn't sound like the son she knew, the one who'd always been focused on profits and returns on investment. "That can't be right."

"I heard it myself. He was quite passionate about it."

She frowned. "Perhaps he's trying to buy goodwill for his development project."

"Or perhaps he genuinely cares about the people here."

She scoffed at the suggestion, but with less certainty than before. "Cliff has always done what's best for Cliff. That's his nature."

"Was that his nature, or was that what you expected of him?" Jonah asked carefully.

The question caught her off guard. "What do you mean?"

"I'm just wondering if perhaps you're seeing what you *expect* to see in your son."

"That's ridiculous," she snapped. "I know my own child."

"Do you? When was the last time you really talked to him? Not argued, not lectured, but talked?" he asked gently.

She fell silent. When indeed? She couldn't remember a conversation with Cliff in years that hadn't devolved into criticism or arguments.

"He was always difficult," she said finally. "Even as a child."

"Difficult children often grow into adults still trying to figure out their place in the world."

She sighed. "When did you become so wise?"

"Around the same time my hair turned gray." He smiled.

But Jonah had never been afraid to approach a problem head-on or to speak honestly. It's one of the many things she admired about him. She sat thinking about his words for a few minutes. The only sound was Winston's gentle snoring and the distant work crews outside.

"I saw him help Beverly with her roof yesterday," Jonah said eventually.

"Beverly let him help her?" That was unexpected. Beverly had made her feelings about Cliff quite clear over the years.

"Apparently, she needed the help and couldn't find anyone else. He was there for hours and came back the next day, according to Darlene. Fixed the whole thing himself."

She thought about the complicated history between her son and Beverly, though she didn't know all the details. She was fairly certain there had been some kind of feelings between the two of them when they were young. But then Cliff had left.

And now he was fixing her roof?

"I just don't know what to make of all this," she admitted.

"Like I said, people can surprise you."

"But is it genuine? That's what I keep wondering." Her fingers resumed their tapping. "Is he really helping because he cares, or is this all some elaborate scheme to win people over to his side?"

"Why can't it be both?" Jonah suggested. "Maybe he does care about the town and also wants to see his project succeed."

"Those two things seem fundamentally at odds."

"Not necessarily. In his mind, maybe that development represents progress for Magnolia Key."

"Progress." She shook her head. "Concrete monstrosities and overcrowding are not progress."

"To you," he pointed out. "But to someone with a different vision for the future, maybe it is."

She hadn't considered the possibility that Cliff might genuinely believe his project was good for the town. She'd assumed his motives were purely selfish.

"It's possible," Jonah continued, "that he's reconnecting with what made Magnolia special to him in the first place. Seeing the community pull together after the hurricane. Maybe he truly cares about the town?"

She considered the question carefully. Did Cliff care about Magnolia Key? He'd certainly shown more concern for its residents in the past week than he had in years. And there was something different about him since the hurricane. Less polished, more genuine.

Jonah leaned forward. "And to be honest, I see a bit of myself in Cliff. Trying to win the respect of the town. Back when we were young, the town and your father held a pretty poor opinion of me. Nothing I could do would change that. Maybe Cliff felt the same thing, and now he's trying to win your approval."

"I don't know." She paused, the confession difficult. "But I've spent so many years being disappointed by him that I'm not sure I can trust what I'm seeing now."

"Or maybe you can. Maybe this is the real Cliff now."

"I do feel like I'm getting to know him a bit better now that he's been staying here with us. But like last night when we were playing cards, I half expected him to cheat to win, but he was a gracious loser when you won the game."

"Maybe it's time to give him the benefit of the doubt," Jonah suggested gently.

"And if I'm wrong? If this is just another one of his schemes?"

"Then at least you'll know you tried." He

reached across and took her hand. "And isn't that worth something?"

She squeezed his hand, grateful for his steady presence in her life. "When did you become such an optimist?"

"I've always been an optimist. How else would I have had the courage to pursue you?" He winked at her.

That brought a genuine smile to her face. "Fair point."

Outside, the sounds of the town rebuilding continued. Hammers and saws, voices calling instructions, the occasional burst of laughter. Magnolia Key was resilient, just as it had always been. Perhaps her son was trying to find his place in all that.

"I'll think about it," she promised, though the thought of changing her stance on Cliff after so many years seemed a bit overwhelming.

"That's all anyone can ask," Jonah said.

CHAPTER 17

That afternoon, Miss Eleanor walked into Coastal Coffee right after closing time while Beverly was clearing up the last tables. "Miss Eleanor, hi. I'm just closing up, but I can get you some coffee. I even have cream now." She smiled.

"I know you're closed, but I just wanted to talk to you without so many people around if you have time."

"I do." She frowned, wondering what the woman needed. "Let me just flip the sign to closed, and I'll get us some coffee."

Miss Eleanor took her usual table, and Beverly came back with coffee and sat down.

She poured coffee into both cups, taking a moment to gather her thoughts. She appreciated the quiet of the cafe after hours, though her usual post-closing routine was now interrupted. She added fresh cream to Miss Eleanor's cup—just the way the older woman liked it—and pushed it across the table.

"Thank you." Miss Eleanor tapped her fingers lightly on the table's edge. "Cliff has been staying with me at Jonah's house."

She nodded, not quite knowing what to say to that. She hadn't expected Miss Eleanor would ever tolerate her son's company for more than a few hours, much less days, now weeks. Nor did she ever think Miss Eleanor would admit she was staying at Jonah's house.

"It's been… interesting," Miss Eleanor continued, her lips pursing slightly. "I'm getting to know Cliff a bit better." She took a slow sip of her coffee. "I heard he even helped with your roof repair."

"He did." She fidgeted with her coffee cup, rotating it in small circles. "I couldn't find a contractor who wasn't already booked solid with post-hurricane work."

"Hmm." Miss Eleanor studied her face with those sharp eyes that seemed to miss nothing. "He's been helping all over town. I didn't expect that."

"Neither did I," she admitted, remembering her own surprise at seeing Cliff with his sleeves rolled up, replacing shingles on her roof. He'd worked efficiently, barely speaking except to ask for tools or to update her on his progress.

Miss Eleanor set her cup down precisely, the small clink against the saucer sounding unnaturally loud in the empty cafe. She looked straight at Beverly and asked, "There was something between you and Cliff all those years ago, wasn't there?"

She froze, her coffee cup halfway to her lips. She set it down carefully, buying herself a few precious seconds to think. The question hung in the air between them, impossible to ignore. How much did she know? How much had she guessed?

"I…" She started, then stopped. She'd never discussed her relationship with Cliff with anyone except Maxine. It had been their secret—hers and Cliff's—all those years ago. But now, with Cliff's mother looking at her expectantly, she wasn't certain how to answer.

"You don't need to protect my feelings, Beverly," she said. "I'm well aware that my son had a life I wasn't privy to. Especially as a teenager."

She took a deep breath. "We were… close for a while." She kept her voice steady, though her heart had picked up its pace. "It was a long time ago."

She nodded. "I suspected as much. I remember how he used to look at you when you both were young." She sighed, a small sound that carried decades of regret. "Theodore and I, we weren't… We weren't good at seeing what was right in front of us sometimes. Or… maybe we ignored what we didn't want to see."

She stared at her coffee, watching the light play across its surface. "I don't think anyone knew. We were pretty careful."

"Because of us," Miss Eleanor stated flatly. It wasn't a question. "Because Theodore and I would have disapproved."

There was no point denying it. "Yes."

"The Whitmores and Griffins have always had certain… expectations. Theodore was even worse about it than I was. Lineage and status meant everything to him."

She'd never heard the woman speak this candidly before. She didn't quite know how to respond.

"I made mistakes with Cliff," Miss Eleanor continued, her voice softer now. "Many mistakes." She looked directly at Beverly. "We pushed him away with all our rules and expectations."

"Miss Eleanor, I—"

"Call me Eleanor, please. I think we're past the formalities at this point."

She nodded, shocked. Though the thought of calling Miss Eleanor by just her first name felt strange after all these years. "Eleanor," she tried. The name felt foreign on her tongue.

"You were close and then… Cliff left suddenly."

She swallowed hard. "Yes."

"He broke your heart, didn't he?"

The blunt question caught her off guard. The

old pain rose up unexpectedly, fresh as if it had happened yesterday instead of decades ago. She wasn't sure how much to share.

"Go on, dear. Tell me."

She looked up at Miss Eleanor—*Eleanor*. "We… we were supposed to meet at the ferry. Run away together." She hadn't planned to share so much, but the words spilled out. "He never showed up. And then I never heard from him again. Well, until he showed up for this development of his."

Eleanor closed her eyes briefly. "I didn't know that part."

"Why are you asking me about this now?"

"Because I'm trying to understand my son. The man he's become. And I'm starting to think I never really knew the boy he was either." She set her cup down with a finality that suggested she'd reached some kind of decision. "I've spent days watching him help people around town. Fixing things. Talking to people—really listening to them. It's not the Cliff I thought I knew."

She considered this. The Cliff who'd fixed her roof had been focused, hardworking, and surprisingly considerate, making sure to clean up after himself and disturb her business as little as possible. It wasn't the entitled developer who'd stood up at the town meeting, insisting his high-rise was the future Magnolia Key needed.

"People change," she offered, not sure if she believed it herself.

"Do they?" Eleanor's face held a look of sadness. "Or do we just finally see parts of them that were there all along?"

"I think…" She hesitated, unsure if she should continue. "I think he always wanted your approval. Even when he was doing everything he could to make you angry."

Eleanor nodded slowly. "Jonah said something similar. It's… difficult to face these things at my age. To realize how much damage I may have done." She straightened her shoulders slightly. "But that's my burden to bear, not yours."

"Why tell me all this?" she asked.

"Because whatever was between you and Cliff isn't entirely in the past, is it?" Eleanor's gaze was piercing again. "I see how you look at him. How he looks at you too."

Heat rose to her cheeks. "That's not—"

"You don't have to explain anything to me," Eleanor interrupted gently. "I just thought you should know that I'm seeing my son differently these days. And perhaps it might be worth your while to do the same."

Beverly didn't know what to say to that. The idea of seeing Cliff differently, of letting go of thirty years of hurt and resentment, felt both impossible and strangely tempting.

"And there's something else you should know. About the night Cliff left town."

"What about that night?" She sat up straighter. She'd spent decades trying not to think about that night, pushing away the memories of standing alone at the ferry landing, clutching a small suitcase, waiting for a boy who never came.

Eleanor took a deep breath, her shoulders rising with the effort. "Theodore and I had an argument that night. A terrible one."

She watched Eleanor's face, noting how the lines around her mouth deepened as she spoke. She'd never seen the woman look so… vulnerable.

"Theodore found out about some trouble Cliff had gotten into. I don't even remember what it was now—something trivial. But Theodore flew into a rage." Eleanor's gaze drifted to the window, looking out at nothing in particular. "He said Cliff was worthless. That he would never amount to anything. That… he regretted the fact we ever had Cliff…"

A chill ran through her. She remembered how Cliff had always craved his father's approval, how devastated he would look after one of Theodore's cutting remarks.

"Theodore stormed out of the house after that. He was gone for hours." Eleanor's voice had dropped even lower, forcing Beverly to lean in to hear her. "I've always feared that Cliff heard us arguing that night. That he heard what his father said about him."

She sat back, stunned by the revelation. "You think that's why he left?"

Eleanor nodded, her eyes suddenly bright with unshed tears. "I've always feared so. The timing… It's too much of a coincidence. He was just… gone the next morning."

She tried to process this new information. All these years, she'd believed Cliff had simply abandoned her, chosen something—or someone—over their plans together.

"Did you ever ask him? About whether he heard you?" she asked.

Eleanor shook her head. "No. By the time I saw him again, years had passed. He was different. Harder. More like his father than I wanted to admit. And I… I was too proud." She gave a small, sad smile. "Another failing of the Whitmores. We excel at pride."

"I always thought…" She hesitated.

"You thought what?"

"I thought he'd found someone else. Or that he just didn't care enough." A weight lifted as she finally voiced the fear she'd carried for so long. "I never considered that he might have left because he felt he wasn't good enough."

Eleanor reached across the table and placed her

hand over hers—another unprecedented gesture. "I failed my son in many ways. But I think one of my greatest failures was not seeing what was happening between you two. Not understanding what you meant to him."

She stared at their hands—Eleanor's thin, age-spotted one covering her own. "I don't know what I meant to him. Not really."

"Well, perhaps that's something you should find out," Eleanor said, withdrawing her hand and straightening in her chair. Some of her usual composure had returned, though her eyes remained softer than Beverly had ever seen them.

She sat in silence, trying to absorb everything Eleanor had shared. Could it really be that Cliff hadn't abandoned her on a whim but had fled from his father's cruel words? Had he truly believed he needed to prove himself before he deserved to be with her?

The pain of that night had shaped her in ways she'd never fully acknowledged. It had made her cautious and reluctant to risk her heart again. And now, with this new understanding about Cliff, she felt as though the ground beneath her beliefs was shifting.

Beverly carried the empty coffee cups to the kitchen, her mind still reeling from Eleanor's revelations. How could one conversation change so much? Thirty years of hurt and assumptions were suddenly cast in a new light, making her question everything she thought she knew about Cliff's departure.

The kitchen door opened, and Maxine walked in. "I just saw Miss Eleanor leaving. She looked… different. Almost emotional. What was that all about?"

She rinsed the cups in the sink and placed them in the dishwasher before turning to her friend. "She came to talk about Cliff."

"Cliff? What about him?" Maxine's eyebrows shot up.

"She told me something I never knew." She stopped cleaning and leaned against the counter. "Something about the night Cliff left town. The night he was supposed to meet me at the ferry."

"You mean when he stood you up and broke your heart?" Maxine's protective tone was familiar. Always on her side.

"It turns out there might have been more to it." Suddenly tired, she walked over and sat down on a chair at the small table in the kitchen. Maxine joined her. "Miss Eleanor—oh, she told me to call her just Eleanor. Can you believe that? Anyway, she said she and Theodore had a terrible argument that night. About Cliff."

"Wait, I'm still dumbfounded that Miss Eleanor told you to call her Eleanor. But, go on."

"According to Eleanor, Theodore said some awful things. That Cliff was worthless. That he'd never amount to anything." Her voice caught. "That he regretted they'd ever had him."

Maxine's hand flew to her mouth. "Oh, wow. That's harsh, even for Mr. Griffin."

"Eleanor thinks Cliff overheard them. She thinks that's why he left so abruptly."

"And never showed up to meet you," Maxine added softly.

She nodded. "Maybe he felt he had to prove himself first. That he wasn't good enough for me."

"That would explain a lot." Maxine moved closer, placing a hand on Beverly's arm. "How do you feel about this?"

"Confused. Sad." She sighed. "For thirty years, I've believed he just didn't care enough. That I wasn't important enough to him."

"And now?"

"Now I don't know what to think. If he really left because of what his father said…" She trailed off, the implications too overwhelming to voice.

"But I still can't get used to you calling her Eleanor."

A small smile tugged at Beverly's lips. "I know. But she was… different today. More vulnerable than I've ever seen her. It's hard to keep calling someone Miss Anything when you've seen them nearly cry."

"Well, I'm shocked." Maxine pretended to fan herself. "You're on a first-name basis with Eleanor Griffin? The Eleanor Griffin? Town matriarch and keeper of all things proper?"

She laughed, grateful for the moment of lightness. "I know. Who would have thought?"

"Do you think I'll ever reach that level of familiarity with her? Should I start practicing? 'Good morning, Eleanor. Lovely weather we're having, Eleanor.'"

Beverly grinned. "I really don't know. She might revoke my privileges if she hears I've been spreading the news."

They both laughed, but her smile faded as her thoughts returned to Cliff. All these years, she'd carried around this story of abandonment, letting it shape her decisions and her heart. What if she'd been wrong? What if Cliff had been carrying his own painful narrative all this time?

"So, what are you going to do?" Maxine asked, reading her thoughts as she often did.

"I don't know that either. I've spent so long believing one version of the story. It's not easy to just… change that."

"But if what Miss Eleanor said is true—"

"Even if it is, it doesn't erase thirty years. It

doesn't change the fact that he never tried to contact me, never explained."

"Maybe he couldn't." Maxine's voice was gentle. "Maybe he was too hurt or too ashamed."

She looked up at her friend. "Maybe. But where does that leave us now?"

CHAPTER 18

Eleanor stood in front of her damaged house as she watched the workers moving at what seemed like a glacial pace. The massive oak that had crashed through her porch had been removed, but the roof repairs were dragging on interminably. She tapped her foot impatiently against the sidewalk.

"Mrs. Griffin, we're making good progress," Hank—was that his name?— called from atop his ladder. "Should have the roof sealed up by tomorrow, weather permitting."

"That's what you said yesterday," she replied tartly. "And the day before."

Hank had the good grace to look sheepish. "Well, ma'am, we found some additional water damage in the joists. Better to do it right than do it twice."

She sighed. Waiting for repairs to get finished

was testing her limits. Three people living in Jonah's small house made her miss her own space and her own routines. Winston seemed perfectly content at Jonah's place, but she wasn't. Though she had to admit she was enjoying Jonah's company.

"I'm going inside to check on things," she announced, not waiting for permission. It was her house, after all.

She carefully stepped around piles of construction materials on the porch, noting with approval that the new boards matched the old ones reasonably well. Inside, the house smelled of dampness despite the dehumidifiers running constantly. The main living areas were relatively untouched by the storm, but upstairs was another story entirely.

She walked through the downstairs rooms, running her fingers along surfaces, grimacing at the fine layer of construction dust that had settled everywhere. Sitting idly by was never her strong suit. She couldn't help with the major repairs, but surely there was something useful she could do.

Her gaze settled on the door to Theodore's office. She hadn't changed a thing in there since he passed away. Each time she'd considered it, something had stopped her. But now, with the rest of the house in disarray, the time seemed right.

She pushed open the door and stepped inside. The room smelled musty, a combination of old books, leather, and something distinctly Theodore. The heavy mahogany desk dominated the space, his reading glasses still perched on top as if he might return any moment to continue reviewing papers.

It took her a moment to notice the damage. Water had seeped down from the ceiling in one corner, affecting the tall bookshelf that housed Theodore's collection of maritime history and law books. Several volumes were visibly warped, their bindings rippled with water damage.

"Well, that settles it," she said aloud to no one in particular. "No sense preserving ruined books."

She located a few empty boxes in the hallway closet and brought them into the office. Starting with the damaged shelf, she began removing books, examining each one before placing it in a box. Some were beyond saving, but most were simply dust-covered and musty.

As she worked, she found herself wondering why she had preserved this room like a museum exhibit all these years. She'd kept everything exactly as he'd left it, right down to the half-empty cup of pencils on his desk.

"All these years," she muttered, shaking her head. "What a waste of a perfectly good room."

She continued methodically emptying the shelves, occasionally pausing to flip through a volume that caught her attention. A book on coastal navigation brought back memories of early marriage years when Theodore would take their boat out on weekends, hosting business associates. He'd never once offered a romantic cruise, just the two of them for some couple time together.

As she reached for a thick volume, a yellowed envelope slipped out and fluttered to the floor. She bent to retrieve it, her joints protesting slightly. Whoever it was addressed to was smeared and unreadable. She stuffed it in her pocket and continued her cleanup.

Each book now represented another piece of the past she could finally release. After filling three boxes with books for donation, she turned her attention to the desk.

The drawers were filled with Theodore's papers. Old bills, correspondence, and boat maintenance records were filed in perfectly organized files. Most could go straight to recycling.

As she worked, her mind kept returning to Cliff. He'd been helping everyone in town since the hurricane, even helping coordinate the repairs to her house. So different from the self-centered behavior she'd expected from him. Perhaps she'd been wrong about his intentions for Magnolia Key as well.

Although, his development plans were still problematic for the town's character. But seeing him pitch in after the storm, reconnecting with neighbors who'd known him since childhood, gave her hope that the boy she'd raised wasn't completely lost beneath the businessman exterior.

By late afternoon, she had cleared most of Theodore's office. The space looked larger without the overstuffed bookshelves, and sunlight streamed through the windows she'd cleaned. She stood in the center of the room, envisioning possibilities. Perhaps a sitting room where she could enjoy morning coffee while watching the birds in the backyard.

She felt lighter somehow, as if clearing the physical items had also cleared something inside her. This room had been a shrine to the past, to a marriage that had been filled with shattered expectations. Now it could become something new, something entirely hers.

"Mrs. Griffin?" Hank's voice rang through the hallway.

"Back here," she called out.

Hank appeared in the doorway. "We're wrapping up for today."

"Okay, thank you."

"And, ma'am, you'll be pleased to know we should be finished with the major repairs by Friday. You'll be back home before you know it."

And those were the words she'd been longing to hear.

After the workers left, to reward herself for a job well done, she headed to the kitchen to make a pot of tea. She put the teakettle on, enjoying the quiet and the space.

The letter in her pocket rustled slightly, and she took it out. Curious, she sat on a chair at the table and carefully opened the envelope.

Her breath caught as she read the words. "Oh, no."

There was no reason Theodore should have had this letter unless… But she couldn't believe he'd be that cruel. Though… maybe she *could* believe it.

She slowly folded the letter and slipped it back into the envelope. It was time for the intended recipient to get this letter. She got up and turned off the teakettle. The letter had been hidden too long to wait for her to sit and drink a cup of tea.

Beverly slid her plate onto the drying rack, enjoying the quiet of her cottage kitchen. After a long day at Coastal Coffee, the simple rhythm of washing dishes soothed her. She'd always found comfort in the ordinary tasks that kept her hands busy while her mind worked through tangled thoughts. And lately, her thoughts had been more snarled than usual.

The hurricane's aftermath continued to keep everyone on Magnolia Key scrambling, but the community had pulled together beautifully. Her cafe had become a gathering spot again. And Cliff—well, Cliff had surprised her. His offer to fix her roof had been genuine, and he'd shown up with tools and materials, working alongside a couple of guys from his crew.

She'd avoided any deep conversation with him, keeping things strictly business. But Eleanor's revelations about the night Cliff left the island had been playing on repeat in her mind.

The sharp knock at her front door startled her from her thoughts. She dried her hands on a dish towel and padded across the living room. Who would be visiting at this hour? Maxine usually called first.

When she opened the door, she blinked in surprise. Eleanor stood on her porch, looking as proper and composed as always, despite the late hour and the chaos of post-hurricane life.

"Eleanor," she said, still not quite used to dropping the "Miss" after all these years. "Is everything all right?"

"We need to talk." Her tone left no room for argument.

She hesitated. She hadn't quite recovered from their last talk, which had upended decades of assumptions about Cliff's departure. Nor had Eleanor ever been inside her home, but something in Eleanor's expression made her step back and gesture to enter.

"Of course. Come in. Would you like some hot tea?" She closed the door, noticing how the woman scanned the cottage with sharp eyes.

"Tea would be nice," Eleanor said, then added, "Your home is lovely. You've done well with it."

The compliment surprised her. Eleanor wasn't known for dispensing praise freely.

"Thank you. Let me put the kettle on."

In the kitchen, she filled her kettle and set out two cups. Eleanor took a seat at the small kitchen table, her back straight, hands folded primly in front of her.

"Have you spoken with Cliff yet?" Eleanor asked without preamble.

She placed tea bags in the cups, buying herself a moment before answering. "No, I haven't. Not about… that."

"I see. May I ask why not?"

She turned to face her. "I'm not sure how to even broach the subject. Would I say something like, by the way, your mother told me your father said terrible things about you the night you left town, and I've been blaming you for standing me up all these years when maybe you had good reason to leave? That doesn't exactly roll off the tongue."

The kettle whistled, and she poured steaming water into the cups.

"Milk? Sugar?" she asked.

"No, thank you."

She set the cups on the table and sat across from Eleanor.

"Maybe this will help." Eleanor reached into her handbag and withdrew a yellowed envelope, placing it carefully on the table between them.

She stared at it. "What is this?"

Eleanor's eyes held a mix of regret and purpose. "A letter. From Cliff to you. Written the night he left."

Her hand trembled slightly as she reached for the envelope. "I don't understand." She opened the envelope and unfolded one section of the letter. Her name was written at the top in handwriting she instantly recognized, even after all these years. Cliff's handwriting. She closed her eyes for a moment.

"I believe that Cliff left this for you, but somehow Theodore found it before you saw it. I guess he followed Cliff that night and… I believe he opened the letter and read it, then took it and hid it in a book in his office. I found it today when I was boxing up his books.

She traced her fingers over her name, written in Cliff's bold, youthful handwriting. "Why would he do that?"

"I can only guess at his reasons, but I suspect he thought he was protecting Cliff. Or punishing him. Maybe both. Theodore had very firm ideas about what was best for our family. About what was best for Cliff." Eleanor's voice turned bitter. "He believed Cliff needed to focus on college, on making something of himself. Not on—"

"A girl from the wrong side of the island?" she finished for her.

"Those were Theodore's views, not mine. Though I admit I didn't do enough to counter them. I'm afraid that worrying about what was proper and what people would think of our family... that has always been my weakness. And I paid dearly for that, both with Cliff and with Jonah."

Eleanor took a sip of her tea and then looked pointedly at her. "Aren't you going to read it?"

She nodded and unfolded the rest of the page, smoothing the paper as her heart pounded.

Beverly,

I'm so sorry to leave tonight after we made plans. My father said some things I overheard, and I needed to leave. I want to prove to my father that I can be a success. Make him proud of me. Make you proud of me, too, I guess.

You can write to me at the address at the bottom of the letter. If I don't hear from you, I'll understand. I know we had plans to leave together, but this is something I have to do.

I do care about you.

~

Love,

Cliff

~

She looked up at Eleanor with tears in her eyes. "He did hear what Theodore said."

Eleanor bobbed her head. "Yes, I was afraid he did."

"He says he was leaving to make a success and prove himself. And… he asked me to write him."

"But of course you never did because Theodore took the letter and hid it."

"All these years…" She trailed off, lost in sadness, lost in knowing how that one night had affected her life so deeply. And all her thoughts about that night… and about Cliff… were so very wrong.

"I've spent too many years watching my son drift through life, never quite connecting with anyone or anything. And I've spent too many years watching you build walls around yourself. Maybe it's time for both of you to know the whole truth and talk about it." Eleanor met her gaze directly. "So, now are you going to go talk to him?"

She looked at the letter again and trailed her fingers over the words "Love, Cliff." A fierce wave of determination swept through her. Now it was her turn to try and make things right.

"Yes. Yes, I am. It's high time that Cliff and I have a serious talk. But then, I don't know what happens next."

"That's for you and Cliff to figure out." Eleanor stood. "I'll leave you to it then."

CHAPTER 19

Beverly left her cottage with the letter in her pocket and drove around town. Her heart felt lighter than it had in years, yet also strangely unsettled. The sun was beginning to set, casting golden light over Magnolia Key's still-damaged streets as she searched for Cliff.

She checked Jonah's house first but only found Jonah tending to his garden. He mentioned Cliff had gone to help with cleanup efforts around town. Next, she tried the hardware store, the park, and even drove past the site where Cliff's controversial development was planned.

No sign of him.

She spotted Cliff's red truck on the side street near the old theater building and pulled over. The historic theater had suffered minor damage during the hurricane. It was mostly water damage from a section of the roof that had leaked. Tori had mentioned she was organizing volunteers to help with repairs.

She crossed the street and tried the front doors, finding them unlocked. The grand old lobby was dim, but she could hear voices and the sound of something being dragged across the floor coming from the main theater.

"Hello?" she called out, her voice echoing slightly in the cavernous space.

"We're in here!" Tori's voice called back.

She made her way through the lobby and pushed open the double doors to the theater. Inside, Tori was supervising as Cliff hauled heavy debris into a pile near the stage. Both were dusty and looked like they'd been working hard all afternoon.

"Beverly." Tori smiled, brushing dust from her hands. "What brings you over here?"

"I was looking for Cliff, actually." The words felt strange coming out of her mouth after so many years of avoiding him.

Cliff stopped what he was doing, surprise evident on his face as he set down the piece of damaged ceiling tile he'd been carrying.

Tori glanced between them, a knowing look passing over her face. "Well, we were just finishing up for the day, anyway. I think we've done all we can until the professional roofers get here tomorrow."

"Are you sure? I don't want to interrupt if you still need help."

"Absolutely," Tori said, already reaching for her jacket. "Cliff has been a tremendous help, but we're done for today." She turned to Cliff. "Thanks again for pitching in. I really appreciate it."

He nodded. "No problem. I'll come back tomorrow to help the roofers if you need me."

"That would be wonderful." They all headed outside, and Tori locked the door. "I'll leave you two to talk." She gave Beverly a supportive smile as she passed.

Once Tori had gone, she and Cliff stood awkwardly on the theater's steps. He looked different somehow. He looked not just older than the boy she'd known, but somehow humbler than the businessman who'd presented his development plans at the town meeting.

"You wanted to talk to me?" he asked, breaking the silence.

"Yes." She took a deep breath. "Would you mind coming over to Coastal Coffee? It's closed now, and we can have some privacy there."

He raised an eyebrow, but nodded. "Sure."

They walked down the street to the cafe, and she used her key to let them in, flipping on just a few lights rather than the full overhead fluorescents.

"Have a seat," she said, gesturing to a table in the back corner. "Can I get you anything?"

Cliff hesitated. "I don't want to put you to any trouble."

"It's no trouble. I have some chocolate cake left over from today."

A boyish grin spread across his face. "Chocolate cake? You wouldn't happen to have some milk to go with it, would you?"

"I think I can manage that," she said, unable to suppress a small smile.

While Cliff settled at the corner table, she went behind the counter. She cut two generous slices of cake, poured two glasses of milk, and carried everything back to the table on a tray.

"This looks great," he said as she set a plate in front of him. He took a bite and grinned. "Delicious."

Silence dropped between them like a wall while they both took nibbled at their cake. Finally, he looked at her. "So… you wanted to talk to me."

Now was the time. No more stalling. Her pulse raced as she reached into her pocket, pulled out the letter, and placed the yellowed envelope on the table between them. Cliff's eyes widened when he saw it.

"Is that what I think it is? You kept it all these years?"

She shook her head slowly. "No, I just received it today."

Confusion crossed his face. "I don't understand.

I left that letter for you the night I... the night I left Magnolia Key."

"I know. But I never got it." She tapped the envelope with her fingertip. "Your father must have found it before I did. He kept it hidden all these years. Your mother found it today while clearing out Theodore's office."

Cliff stared at the envelope, his fork forgotten halfway to his mouth. "My father took it? All this time, I thought..." He set his fork down, his appetite apparently gone. "I thought you got the letter and chose not to write to me."

"And I thought you left without a word, that you didn't care enough to say goodbye."

They sat in silence for a moment, both processing the magnitude of all the misunderstandings that had shaped their lives.

"May I?" Cliff gestured toward the letter.

She nodded, and he picked up the envelope, carefully extracting the letter he'd written decades ago. His eyes moved across the page, reading his own youthful words.

"I remember... I remember writing this," he said finally. "I was so crushed after overhearing my father. The things he said about me..." He folded the letter and slid it back into the envelope. "I wanted to prove him wrong so badly."

"Did you?" she asked quietly. "Prove him wrong?"

His expression turned pensive. "In some ways. I made money. Built a successful business. But in other ways…" He shook his head. "Maybe he was right about some things. I've spent my life chasing success without stopping to think about what really matters."

She took a sip of her milk, gathering her thoughts. "Your mother told me what Theodore said that night. That you'd never amount to anything."

"Yeah, well, dear old Dad never did think much of me." His tone was bitter, but there was resignation in it too. "I always thought if I just made enough money, built enough buildings, he'd finally see I was worth something."

"And now? Do you still feel that way?"

He looked around the coffee shop, his gaze thoughtful. "Coming back home has made me realize how empty all that success felt. This place…" He gestured around them. "Magnolia Key hasn't changed that much. It still feels like home, somehow."

"Yet you want to change it with your development," she pointed out, unable to stop herself but trying to keep the accusation from her voice.

"I thought I was helping," he said simply. "Bringing jobs, progress. But maybe I was still just trying to prove something." He looked directly at her. "Beverly, if I'd known you never got that letter…"

She waited, her heart beating faster.

"What would you have done if you had received it?" he asked instead.

She looked down at her barely touched cake. "I would have written back," she admitted. "I was hurt and angry when you didn't show up, but if I'd known why… yes, I would have written."

"And I would have come back for you," he said softly. "Eventually. When I had something to offer."

The finality of might-have-beens settled over them, and the decades of separate lives that might have been shared.

"What happens now?" she asked.

"I don't know," Cliff admitted. "But I'm glad you came to find me today. Glad we finally know the truth."

"I am too."

"Can I ask you something?" Cliff looked directly into her eyes.

"Of course."

"How do you feel about me now?"

She paused, considering her words. "I'm… I'm really not sure. I've had years of, um, *disliking* you strongly."

"I'm sure you did. I'm sorry you didn't at least get my letter."

"That's not your fault."

"No, but I should have come to find you before I left. Not just left the letter." He frowned. "I was just so… hurt by my father's words."

"There are many things I wish had gone differently, but we can't change the past."

"No, we can't." He reached over and took her hand. "Do you think we can go back to being friends? I've missed you."

She looked down at their hands, entangled again after all these years. "Yes, I think we can be friends. That's a good place to start."

CHAPTER 20

Maxine came behind the counter where Beverly was rolling silverware into napkin rolls. She playfully bumped Beverly's shoulder. "Just saw Cliff leave. Looks like it's becoming a daily habit for him to come in for breakfast. He's been in every single day this week."

"Oh, has he? I hadn't noticed." She tried to look innocent. Or believable. But her friend was having none of it.

Maxine rolled her eyes. "And he comes at the end of the breakfast rush so you'll have time to sit and have a cup of coffee with him."

"Okay, yes, he does."

She watched Maxine's knowing smile with a mixture of amusement and mild embarrassment. She couldn't deny it anymore—she and Cliff had fallen into a comfortable routine over the past week.

Every morning after the breakfast rush, he'd come in, they'd share coffee, and talk about everything from town gossip to their shared memories.

"And because I know you'll find out anyway, we had dinner at Sharky's last night. But we're just friends."

Maxine had begun to warm up to Cliff now, ever since Beverly told her all about what had happened the night Cliff left and the letter she'd never received. That conversation had been emotional—Maxine listening with wide eyes as she explained about Theodore's interference and how Eleanor had found the letter.

"I'm just glad you two are talking," Maxine said, grabbing a stack of napkins to help. "The way you used to glare at him when he walked in here, I thought the coffee might curdle."

She laughed. "I wasn't that bad."

"You absolutely were. But I get it now. Finding out the truth changes things."

She nodded, feeling a wave of gratitude for her friend's understanding. Unlike Eleanor, who seemed to have done a complete turnaround on Cliff, suggesting they pick up right where they left off decades ago, Maxine understood Beverly needed time.

"I'm still getting used to the idea of having Cliff as a friend. For so many years, I either missed him terribly or was furious with him. Now I don't know exactly what to feel."

"I bet. It's been a roller coaster, hasn't it?"

She set down the silverware roll she'd just finished and looked up at Maxine. "It's strange how quickly things can change. A month ago, I couldn't stand the sight of him. Now we're having dinner and talking about old times like the last thirty years never happened."

"But they did happen," Maxine pointed out. "You both lived whole lives apart. That doesn't just disappear because you found out he didn't actually stand you up."

"I know. Sometimes when we're talking, it's like we're those teenagers again. Then he'll mention something about his time in Chicago or one of his development projects, and suddenly I remember we're practically strangers now."

Maxine arranged the silverware rolls in the container on the counter. "So what do you talk about at these daily coffee meetings?"

She smiled. "Everything. Nothing. He tells me about the repairs he's helping with around town. I tell him about the cafe. We talk about the bridge construction—or lack thereof. Sometimes we just sit in comfortable silence."

"And the development project? You two discuss that?"

"Not really," she admitted. "We've agreed to disagree on that for now."

"Just be careful, okay? Friend or not, he's still Cliff Griffin. Don't rush into anything."

She nodded, appreciating her friend's concern. "I'm taking it one coffee at a time."

The bell over the door jingled as a customer entered, and Beverly straightened up, automatically reaching for her order pad. But it was just Dale, coming to meet Maxine for an early lunch.

"Ladies," Dale said with a smile. "Hope I'm not interrupting."

"Not at all," she said. "Your timing is perfect. I was just about to kick this one out from behind my counter. Employees only back here. And Maxine was supposed to be off the clock fifteen minutes ago."

Maxine made a face at Beverly before coming around the counter and kissing Dale on the cheek. "I was helping, thank you very much."

"And gossiping," she added with a grin.

"That's a bonus service I provide." Maxine hung up her apron. "Free of charge."

"Oh, Dale," Beverly said, suddenly remembering. "Before we were all running around preparing for the hurricane, you were telling us something about Vera and Lawrence. Something you'd discovered?"

Dale's eyes lit up the way they always did when

someone mentioned Magnolia Key's history. He settled on a stool at the counter, leaning forward with enthusiasm.

"That's right! I'd almost forgotten with all the storm chaos." He ran a hand through his hair. "I've been looking through some old correspondence that mentioned Eleanor's great-aunt, Vera Whitmore."

"And?"

"Well, I've been trying to confirm the connection between Vera and Lawrence—you know, the prince." Dale's eyes shone with excitement. "I believe there is more to the story than we realized."

She placed the last of the silverware rolls in the container and came around the counter to join them. "Really? What makes you think that?"

"Several things. The timing of her trips abroad, references in other letters I've found at the historical society, and some old newspaper clippings that mention a foreign visitor to Magnolia Key around that time." Dale shrugged. "But I need more concrete evidence before I bring it to Miss Eleanor."

"Have you made any progress?" She had to admit, the mystery of Vera and her prince had fascinated her ever since they'd started finding out information about them.

"I've sent off some emails now that things have settled down after the hurricane," Dale explained. "There's an archive that might have Lawrence's personal papers. And I've requested access to some shipping manifests from that era to verify travel dates. Oh, I've emailed a few newspapers in Europe for some information from their database of past articles."

Maxine grinned and patted Dale's hand affectionately. "You know how Dale likes to cross his T's and dot his I's when he's doing historical research on Magnolia Key."

She smiled, remembering how Dale's passion for history had helped them uncover so many stories about their town. "Well, if anyone can piece together more of Vera and Prince Lawrence's story, it's you."

"I just don't want to tell Miss Eleanor anything until I'm certain," Dale said. "She seems quite protective of her family's history. I want to respect that by getting my facts straight first."

"That's probably wise. Eleanor has strong feelings about her family's legacy."

"Speaking of Miss Eleanor," Maxine said, "how is she doing with the repairs to her house? Is she still staying at Jonah's?"

She nodded, grateful for the change in subject. As fascinating as Vera and Lawrence's story was, it brought up thoughts of lost love and missed opportunities—star-crossed lovers—and that hit a little too close to home these days with Cliff back in her life.

"The repairs are coming along," she said. "I think she's enjoying staying with Jonah more than she lets on. Though she checks on the progress at her house every day."

"Those two are good for each other," Dale observed.

She agreed. Finding a second chance at love later in life had given Eleanor a softer edge. Even Cliff and his mother seemed to be growing closer.

"Well, I should get back to work," Beverly said, glancing at her watch. The lunch crowd would be arriving soon, and there was still prep to do. "Let me know if you find out anything more about Vera and Lawrence."

Dale nodded. "You'll be the first to know—after the proper fact-checking, of course."

CHAPTER 21

Beverly watched the hands of the clock tick past four. The closed sign was in the window, and she mentally ticked through her closing checklist, perfected over the years.

The bell over the door jingled, and she looked up to see Cliff walk in. Her heart did that ridiculous little flutter that it had started doing whenever he appeared. Ever since they'd cleared the air about his letter, things had been different between them—not quite what they'd had as teenagers, but something new, something better in many ways.

"Hey," he said, approaching the counter with that easy smile of his.

"Hey, yourself." She set aside her cleaning cloth. "Coffee?"

"No, I'm good, thanks." He glanced around the

empty shop. "I was actually wondering if I could walk you home when you're done here."

The request was simple enough, but it felt significant somehow. They'd been rebuilding their friendship carefully, step by step, over coffee conversations and casual run-ins around town. This felt deliberate.

"Sure," she said, trying to sound casual herself. "I'm almost finished closing up, if you don't mind waiting."

"Not at all." He settled at the counter, watching as she finished her closing routine.

Beverly moved efficiently through her tasks, all too aware of Cliff's presence. She prepped the coffee makers for tomorrow morning and straightened the chairs at the tables. All the while, she felt Cliff's eyes on her, observing her in her element. It wasn't uncomfortable—rather, the opposite. There was something comforting about his quiet presence.

She came back to the counter and took off her apron.

"Ready?" he asked.

She nodded, and they stepped outside into the late afternoon sunshine. A magical light had that golden quality that made everything on Magnolia Key look like it belonged in a painting.

They walked in companionable silence for a few minutes, their footsteps falling into an easy rhythm on the sidewalk. The storm had left its mark on the town—there were still tarps on some roofs and construction debris in piles waiting to be hauled away—but recovery was happening all around them.

"How's the theater coming along?" she asked, breaking the silence.

"Good. We got the roof finished yesterday. The water damage inside is going to take longer, but at least it's dry now."

"That's wonderful. Tori must be relieved."

"She is. She's already talking about what shows she wants to put on once it's all fixed up."

She smiled. "That sounds like Tori."

They turned onto her street, and she found herself walking a little slower, not quite ready for their time together to end.

"How about you come in for a little while?" The words were out before she'd fully thought them through. "I've got a bottle of wine I've been saving for a special occasion."

He raised an eyebrow. "And this is a special occasion?"

She felt her cheeks warm. "Well, the island's still standing after a hurricane. My roof's fixed. And…" She hesitated, then continued, "And we're friends again. That seems pretty special to me."

His smile softened. "It is. And I'd love to come in."

They climbed the steps to her porch, and she unlocked the door. The cottage welcomed them with its familiar coziness. She moved to the kitchen while Cliff waited in the living room. As she returned, she saw him taking in the photos on her walls and the books on her shelves.

She nodded toward the porch. "It's nice enough to sit outside, don't you think?"

They settled into the wicker chairs on her porch, a gentle breeze rustling the palm fronds in her yard. For a moment, they simply sipped their wine, enjoying the peace of the early evening.

"I heard something interesting…" she said finally, turning to look at him.

"Oh?"

"Mm-hmm. I heard that someone started a hurricane recovery fund for families on the island who don't have insurance or enough savings to repair their homes." She watched his expression carefully. "I heard that someone donated a substantial amount to get it started and has been quietly organizing volunteers to help with repairs."

He shifted in his chair, looking slightly uncomfortable. "Is that right?"

"That's what I heard," she confirmed. "And apparently this mysterious benefactor specifically asked not to be named."

He took a long sip of his wine. "People like to talk in small towns."

"They do," she agreed. "Especially when someone who's been away for a long time comes back and starts doing good things for the community."

His eyes met hers. "It's not a big deal."

"I think it is," she said gently. "Why don't you want people to know?"

He sighed and set his glass down on the small table between them. "Because I don't want it to look like I'm trying to buy goodwill for my development project."

"Is that what you're doing?"

"No." His response was immediate and firm. "The hurricane changed things. Seeing what this community went through, how everyone pulled together…" He shook his head. "I realized that whatever happens with the development, these are good people who need help now."

She nodded as a warmth spread through her that had nothing to do with the wine.

"The fund is one thing," he continued. "But honestly, it needs more money than what I've been able to put in. There are at least eight families who need significant help, and there's only so much I can do."

"Have you thought about doing a fundraiser?" she asked.

He chuckled. "About a hundred times. But I don't know the first thing about organizing something like that. Corporate events, sure. But a community fundraiser?" He shook his head. "That's not my territory."

She gave him a little smile. "It's mine, though."

"What do you mean?"

"I mean, I've helped organize events for the town before. The summer festival, the Christmas market, that sort of thing." She set her glass down. "I could help you put together a fundraiser for the recovery fund."

He looked at her with surprise. "You'd do that?"

"Of course I would. This town is my home. And those families need help. I could ask Tori if we could do it at the theater," she continued, the ideas already forming in her mind. "Once the basic repairs are done. Tori would love to host something like that—it would be a perfect way to reintroduce the space to the community."

"That's… actually a really good idea," he said, leaning forward in his chair. "We could get local businesses to donate items for a silent auction. Maybe have some local musicians perform."

"Exactly!" A spark of excitement gathered inside her. "And food—we could get several restaurants involved. People are always more generous on a full stomach."

"So you'll really help me with this?"

"I will," she said, meeting his eyes. "For Magnolia Key." But it was more than that. It was also to help Cliff. To show him she believed in him.

She believed in him? That thought sent a shockwave through her. So, so very much had changed.

"For Magnolia Key," he echoed, raising his glass in a small toast.

They sat in comfortable silence for a moment, both lost in thoughts about the fundraiser. The sunset painted the sky in shades of orange and pink, with a slash of purple above them. She realized with a start that this was the most relaxed she'd felt in a long time—sitting here with Cliff, planning something good for their community.

"We should probably start making a list," she said eventually. "Figure out what businesses to approach, what kind of timeline we're looking at."

"Some things never change. Always the planner." He winked at her.

"Someone has to be," she retorted, softening the words with a grin.

Cliff stood at Beverly's door, the evening air warm around them. The sound of waves in the distance mingled with a lone gull calling from the sky. The stars began to twinkle above them. He felt a pull toward her he couldn't deny, an undercurrent that had been there since he'd returned to Magnolia Key.

"I'm glad we're back on track." The words tumbling out awkwardly, and he grimaced inwardly at how formal they sounded. "I mean, I'm glad you're not still mad at me."

Her eyes caught his, and for a moment, he saw something there—a flicker of the past, perhaps, or maybe something new. Her lips curved into a soft smile that made his heart beat faster. He took her hand, feeling the warmth of her skin against his.

His gaze dropped to her lips. They were just inches away. One small movement and he could finally have the kiss he'd thought about for decades. The one that had haunted his dreams, the possibility that had lived in a corner of his mind all these years.

His heartbeat quickened. The moment stretched between them, filled with possibility. But something held him back—uncertainty, fear of rejection, or maybe their complicated history. Whatever it was, it kept him rooted in place.

"Goodnight, Beverly," he said finally, giving her hand a gentle squeeze before letting go. "Thanks for the wine. And for agreeing to help with the fundraiser."

Her smile didn't falter, but he thought he saw a hint of disappointment in her eyes. Or was he just projecting his own feelings?

"Goodnight, Cliff," she said softly. "See you tomorrow."

He walked down the steps of her porch. The door closed behind him with a quiet click that somehow felt louder than it should have.

"Idiot," he muttered to himself as he walked along the quiet streets of Magnolia Key.

The neighborhood was peaceful at this hour. Most homes still had lights on, people settling in for the evening after another day of hurricane recovery. He passed Mrs. Henderson's place, noticing her new wind chimes tinkling in the breeze, replacing the ones lost in the storm.

What was wrong with him? He'd waited thirty years for that moment. Thirty years wondering what might have been if his father hadn't crushed his spirit that night, if Theodore hadn't intercepted his letter.

And now, when the perfect opportunity presented itself, he'd choked.

The streetlights cast long shadows as he walked. Jonah's cottage wasn't far, but tonight, the distance felt longer, each step a taunting reminder of his cowardice.

"You're not seventeen anymore," he told himself. "You're a grown man who builds striking buildings for a living. You make million-dollar decisions without blinking. And you can't even kiss a woman you've known your whole life?"

But that was just it. Beverly wasn't just any woman. She was Beverly. The girl who'd helped him through algebra. The teenager who'd listened to his dreams. The woman who'd looked at him with such hurt and betrayal when he returned to Magnolia Key with plans to change her beloved town.

The same woman who now knew the truth and had somehow found it in her heart to forgive him.

He turned onto Wisteria Street, Jonah's cottage now visible ahead. The lights were still on, which meant his mother and Jonah were probably playing cards in the living room, as had become their nightly ritual.

Cliff slowed his pace, not quite ready to face his mother's perceptive gaze. She'd know something was up the minute he walked in. Eleanor Griffin hadn't raised a son without learning to read his every expression. And now that they were actually talking—really talking—for the first time in decades, he found her attention both welcome and unsettling.

He stopped and looked back in the direction of Beverly's cottage. Maybe he should turn around. Go back. Finish what he'd started. Or at least what he'd thought about starting.

No. That would be even more awkward. Showing up at her door again minutes after leaving? What would he say? "Sorry, I forgot to kiss you good night"?

He shook his head and continued toward

Jonah's cottage. The porch light welcomed him, just as it had every night since the hurricane. He'd initially balked at staying with his mother and Jonah, but now he had to admit it wasn't half bad. Jonah was easy to be around, and his mother… well, they were both trying. That counted for something.

As he climbed the steps to Jonah's porch, Cliff realized something. For the first time in years, Magnolia Key felt like home again. Not just a place from his past or a location for his next development, but home. The people, the streets, the smell of the ocean, and yes, Beverly—all of it wrapped around him like a familiar blanket.

And that realization scared him more than he cared to admit.

What if his development project really did change the character of this place? What if Beverly was right all along? What if his mother was right?

He paused at the door, hand on the knob. These were questions for another day. Tonight, he just needed to get through an evening of cards with his mother and Jonah without revealing that he'd almost kissed Beverly Mooney and then chickened out like a teenager.

As he opened the door, he wondered if maybe, just maybe, he'd get another chance… but would he chicken out again?

CHAPTER 22

Beverly lifted her head as the bell over the door jingled, and she smiled. Eleanor entered with Jonah at her side, his hand resting gently at the small of her back. They made their way to Eleanor's usual corner table.

Every Tuesday, for as long as Beverly could remember, Eleanor arrived for breakfast and sat at the same table. But now Jonah joined her. The change in routine might have seemed small to others, but in Magnolia Key, where traditions were as predictable as the tides, it felt significant.

"Good morning, Beverly," Eleanor called, settling herself into her chair.

"Morning, Eleanor. Jonah." Beverly grabbed two menus and headed their way.

Eleanor waved off the menus. "No need. I'll have my usual, and Jonah will have—"

"The veggie omelet with wheat toast," he finished, smiling at Beverly.

She nodded, tucking the menus under her arm. "Coffee for both?"

"Please," they answered in unison, then exchanged a glance that made Beverly feel like she was intruding on something private.

She returned with coffee, two mugs, and cream for Eleanor.

"Thank you, dear." Eleanor nodded.

"It's nice to see you two enjoying breakfast together."

Eleanor's cheeks colored slightly. "Well, it made sense. Jonah's been so kind, letting Cliff and me stay with him while the repairs are being done. It's the least I can do to treat him to breakfast."

"Ellie," Jonah said gently, "you don't need to explain having breakfast with me."

Her blush deepened, and Beverly had to bite back a smile. She'd never seen Miss Eleanor—*no, Eleanor*—looking so flustered.

"And how are the plans coming for the fundraiser?" Jonah asked, steering the conversation in a new direction.

"Really well." She poured their coffee. "Tori is letting us use the theater next Saturday. Cliff's been amazing at getting donations for the silent auction."

The door chimed again, and she glanced over to

see Dale rushing in, his hair windblown and eyes wide with excitement.

"There you are!" he called out, spotting Eleanor. "I knew I'd find you here. I need to talk to you."

Eleanor set down her coffee cup. "Dale, we're having breakfast."

"It's about Vera," Dale said, slightly out of breath but keeping his voice low. "And Prince Lawrence."

Eleanor's expression changed, and she straightened in her chair. "Well, don't just stand there. Join us."

Dale pulled out a chair at their table and sat down, nodding hello to Beverly and Jonah.

"What have you found?" Eleanor asked.

Dale pulled a folder from his messenger bag and extracted a piece of paper. "This," he said, sliding it across the table. "Look, that's Vera. And Prince Lawrence."

Eleanor picked up the paper. She studied it closely, her eyes narrowing as she examined the image. After a long moment, she nodded. "Yes, that's Vera."

Beverly leaned in to get a better look. The black-and-white photograph showed a young woman in an elegant dress standing beside a handsome man in formal attire. They were posed in front of what looked like a castle.

"Where did you find this?" Eleanor asked, still staring at the photo.

"I was actually doing some research on castles in Switzerland, nothing to do with Magnolia Key's history. But I came upon an article from a paper in Switzerland." Dale's eyes were bright with excitement. "I emailed the paper, and they sent me this copy of a photo from their archive. The caption identifies her as Miss Vera Whitmore of Magnolia Key and him as His Royal Highness, Prince Lawrence of Bardonzia."

"What year was this?"

"Nineteen-thirty-five. And once I knew the location, I did some more digging. Your great-aunt Vera and Lawrence lived in Switzerland in that castle you see behind them in the photo." He paused. "And they both died in Switzerland many years later."

"But what about Lawrence's wife? And wasn't he to become king of Bardonzia?"

"His wife died of influenza, in nineteen-thirty."

"But he was king, wasn't he? Why would he move to Switzerland?"

"He never became king. He gave up his birthright, and his brother became king after their father died."

"He gave up all that for Vera?"

Dale nodded. "He did. He must have loved her very much. And they got married." He dug in his bag again. "Look, here's a photo from their wedding."

Eleanor stared at the photo. "My family sent her away, practically exiled her, when there were rumors about her and Lawrence. They couldn't abide with talk about the Whitmore name. It's no wonder she never contacted us to let us know where she was or that she was happily married to Lawrence."

Beverly watched as Eleanor's fingers traced the outlines of the figures in the photograph. The older woman's expression softened, and for a moment, she saw something unexpected in Eleanor's eyes— was it wistfulness?

"I should go get your food," Beverly said, feeling like an intruder in their moment. She hurried to the kitchen, and when she returned, Dale was gone. Eleanor was sitting quietly, and Jonah was sipping his coffee.

"You okay, Eleanor?" she asked as she placed their food on the table.

Eleanor nodded thoughtfully. "I am. After all these years, I finally know that Vera had her happy ending."

Eleanor walked beside Jonah along the sunlit sidewalks back to his cottage. Jonah unlocked the door and held it for her. Winston trotted up to meet them, then immediately headed to his bed in the corner of the living room. She smiled as the dog turned in three circles before settling down with a contented sigh. At least that was a familiar routine.

"Would you like some tea?" Jonah asked, heading toward the kitchen.

"That sounds lovely." She sat on the comfortable armchair by the window, feeling unsettled.

Jonah returned a few minutes later with two steaming mugs of tea and handed one to her. "Sorry, I don't have fancy teacups like you have at your home. But don't worry, we'll get you settled back home in a few days."

It surprised her that she no longer longed to move back into her home where she lived alone with Winston. She'd gotten used to quiet mornings with Jonah and playing card games with Cliff at night.

Jonah sat down in the chair opposite her and studied her face. "You were quiet on the walk home. Are you okay?" he asked, concern etching his features.

She took a sip of her tea before looking up at him. "I am. Just… thoughtful."

"About what?"

She set her mug down on the small wooden table beside her. "About so many things. About Vera. About all the pieces we've found out about her over the months."

"It has been quite the trail of breadcrumbs, hasn't it?"

She nodded. "First, there was that rolled canvas Beverly found in her office—the painting of Bardonzia. How strange that something so significant was tucked away and forgotten all these years."

"And you said Maxine found the coded letter from Vera in an old purse," Jonah added.

"Yes. Then they found Vera's pendant at Tori's theater during the renovations and the hidden letters from Lawrence under the floor of Jenna's cottage, the cottage Vera used to live in."

She sipped on her tea for a few moments. "And then the letter from Lawrence to Vera that was found hidden at Darlene's B&B. All these little pieces of their story scattered across our island like a treasure hunt… like it was meant for us—for me—to find. To finally find out the truth about Vera."

"Maybe it was fate poking you in the right direction."

Eleanor stood and walked to the window, gazing out at Jonah's garden. "I've always wondered what happened to Vera, you know. All these years, I pictured her living out her life lonely, all alone." She turned back to face Jonah. "The Whitmores didn't speak of her much, if ever. There was always this… shadow over her memory. This sense that she'd done something inappropriate by falling in love with Lawrence."

"Times were different then," Jonah said gently.

"Yes, they were. The family thought she'd tarnished the Whitmore name with all those rumors about her and Lawrence. But no matter how the family insisted she marry one of the so-called proper men her father paraded before her, she refused."

"She sounds like a strong, determined woman."

"I admire her so much. I wish…" She turned to Jonah. "I wish I'd been as strong as she was. That I would have chosen you."

"Ah, Ellie, we can't change the past."

"No, we can't. But I wish I could change what my family did to her. Sending her away. I never saw her again. But now…" A smile tugged at her lips. "Now I know she and Lawrence found each other again. Despite everything, despite everyone who tried to keep them apart."

Jonah rose and joined her by the window, wrapping his arm around her shoulders. "And she lived happily ever after with her prince," he quipped with a grin.

She leaned into him, feeling his warmth against her. "Yes, she did. In a castle, no less."

Jonah turned her around to face him. "You know, I think people should always believe in what their heart is telling them. Like I think we should,

Ellie. We've gotten to know each other better with you staying here in my home since the hurricane. We've gotten to know the people we've become. And… I don't want to live without you, Ellie. Without seeing you first thing every morning and last thing every night."

Her heart seemed to freeze in her chest as his words sank in. She stared at him, her mind spinning with a thousand thoughts as he lowered himself to one knee before her. He looked up at her with such openness, such vulnerability.

"Will you marry me, Ellie?"

The world around her seemed to go silent. Even Winston lifted his head from his bed in the corner, watching them with curious eyes. Her hand fluttered to her chest.

Marriage. At her age. It seemed almost absurd —and yet, looking down at Jonah, his eyes filled with hope and love, it felt utterly right.

"I…" she began, her voice catching. She cleared her throat and tried again. "Jonah, are you certain? We're hardly young anymore."

His smile widened. "Which means we don't have time to waste, do we now?"

She couldn't help the small laugh that escaped her lips. "I suppose that's true."

"We've already wasted decades, Ellie," he said, his voice soft but steady. "I don't want to waste a single day more."

She felt an unexpected prickling of tears in her eyes. It had been so long since she'd allowed herself to be truly vulnerable with someone. With Theodore, there had been walls she'd maintained, standards she'd felt compelled to uphold as a Whitmore.

"But at our age? What will people say?" she murmured, but the question lacked conviction even to her own ears.

He reached up and took her hand in his. "Since when does Eleanor Griffin care what people say?"

"Eleanor Griffin has always cared what people say," she admitted, surprising herself with her candor. "Perhaps too much."

She glanced toward the window again, thinking of Vera—of her bravery, her determination to follow her heart despite what her family thought, despite what society expected. All these years, Eleanor had believed that Vera had paid a price for that courage. But now she knew the truth. Vera hadn't paid a price at all—she'd claimed a reward.

"You know," she said softly, turning back to Jonah, "when I first heard what Dale discovered about Vera and Lawrence—that they had reunited and spent their lives together—I felt something I hadn't expected."

"What was that?"

"Envy," she admitted. "All these years, I thought I was the sensible one. The proper Whitmore woman who did what was expected of her. Who married well and upheld the family name. But Vera… Vera was the brave one."

Jonah squeezed her hand gently. "It's not too late for us to be brave, Ellie."

She looked down at their joined hands, at the age spots and wrinkles that marked decades of lived experiences. Decades spent apart when they might have been together.

"If Vera could be brave enough to chase after her dreams," she said slowly, "then so can I. We Whitmore women are strong women, after all."

She took a deep breath, feeling as though she was stepping onto a bridge she couldn't see the end of but knowing, somehow, that Jonah would be waiting for her on the other side.

"Yes," she said, her voice growing stronger. "Yes, Jonah Burton, I will marry you."

The joy that spread across his face was like sunshine breaking through clouds after a long winter storm. He rose, somewhat stiffly—they were neither of them young anymore, after all—and pulled her into his arms.

"You've made me the happiest man in Magnolia Key," he whispered against her hair.

She allowed herself to sink into his embrace, to feel the solid warmth of him against her. It felt like coming home after a long journey—familiar and yet somehow new.

"I don't have a ring," he said as he drew back slightly. "I hadn't planned this, not exactly. It just felt right in this moment."

She smiled. "I don't need a ring, Jonah."

"But I want to give you one," he insisted. "Something worthy of you."

She shook her head slightly. "Nothing too ostentatious, please. I'm not as young as I once was. I'd look ridiculous with some enormous diamond weighing down my hand."

He laughed. "Always practical, my Ellie." His expression softened. "But you must allow me some small romantic gestures. It's been a long time since I've had someone to spoil."

She felt a blush rise to her cheeks. "I suppose I can allow that," she said, trying to maintain her dignified demeanor but failing as a smile crept across her face.

Winston chose that moment to pad over to them, nudging his nose against their legs as if sensing the shift in atmosphere. She bent down to pat him.

"What do you think of this development, Winston?" she asked the dog. "Are you prepared for all this?"

Jonah chuckled. "I think Winston and I have come to an understanding during your stay here. Haven't we, old boy?"

The dog wagged his tail, looking up at them both with what she could have sworn was approval.

"When shall we tell the others?" Jonah asked as they moved to sit on the sofa, still holding hands like teenagers.

She considered the question. "Soon," she decided. "But perhaps we could keep it just between us for a day or two? I'd like to enjoy this moment before the town gossip mill gets hold of it."

"Whatever you want, Ellie." His eyes crinkled at the corners as he smiled. "Although I can't promise I won't be grinning like a fool whenever I see you in public. People might start to wonder."

She laughed softly. "Let them wonder. It might do this town good to have something to speculate about besides hurricane damage and Cliff's development plans." At the mention of her son, a shadow of concern crossed her face. "Cliff," she murmured. "I'll need to tell him, of course."

"Are you worried about his reaction?"

She considered the question. "No," she said after a moment. "Not worried, precisely. But things between us have been changing lately. In a good way, I think. This will be one more change for him to adjust to."

"He wants you to be happy, Ellie. I'm sure of it."

She nodded slowly. "Yes, I believe you're right. And I think—I hope—that he's finding his own path to happiness as well."

"With Beverly, perhaps?" Jonah's eyes twinkled. "I want everyone to find what we have."

"Perhaps. They've certainly been spending a great deal of time together lately."

"Planning that hurricane relief fundraiser."

"Yes, for now, that's what they're calling it," she replied dryly. "But I've seen the way they look at each other when they think no one is watching."

Jonah squeezed her hand. "Like the way I look at you, I imagine."

She felt that unfamiliar blush creep up her cheeks again. "Jonah Burton, you're making me feel like a schoolgirl."

"Good," he said simply, leaning in to place a soft kiss on her lips. "Because you make me feel like the luckiest man alive."

As she returned his kiss, she silently thanked Vera—for her courage, for her example, and for showing Eleanor that it was never too late to follow your heart.

CHAPTER 23

Cliff stepped out of the bathroom, freshly showered and eager to get his day started. The past several weeks had shown him how much the town needed help after the hurricane, and there was still plenty to do. Yesterday, he promised Tori he'd help at the theater, and after that, he planned to check on the community center's roof.

Living under the same roof as his mother and Jonah was proving less uncomfortable than he'd expected. Jonah kept a well-stocked refrigerator, and the cottage was large enough that they weren't constantly bumping into each other. Plus, they'd all been so busy with hurricane recovery that their paths rarely crossed except at dinner.

He grabbed his wallet and keys from the dresser in the guest room and headed for the front door.

The smell of coffee wafted from the kitchen, but he planned to grab some at Coastal Coffee on his way to the theater. The thought of seeing Beverly made him smile.

"Cliff? Do you have a moment before you leave?"

His mother's voice stopped him as he reached for the doorknob. He turned to see her standing in the hallway, a coffee mug clasped in both hands. She was already dressed in her usual impeccable style, despite the early hour.

"Sure, Mother." He braced himself, assuming she wanted to discuss his development project again. Rumors were flying that the planning committee was split on the issue, and he'd heard there would be another town meeting for more public comments. He prepared himself for another round of her disapproval.

She gestured toward the living room. "Can we sit down?"

That caught him off guard. Usually, when his mother wanted to lecture him, she did it standing, looking down her nose at him like he was still twelve years old. He followed her into the living room and settled on the couch while she perched on the edge of an armchair.

"Is something wrong?" he asked.

"No." She set her coffee cup on a coaster.

"Nothing's wrong. I simply wanted to tell you something important."

He waited, studying her face. She looked nervous, which was unlike her. His mother never showed uncertainty about anything.

"Jonah has asked me to marry him," she said. "And I've accepted."

The news hit him like a punch to the chest. Not because he was upset, but because it was so unexpected. His mother—remarrying? After all these years?

"Are you going to say anything?" she asked, her voice betraying a hint of uneasiness he'd rarely heard.

"I'm just surprised," he admitted. "When did this happen?"

"He asked me yesterday. We've been… close… for some time now."

He nodded slowly. "I suspected as much." He'd noticed the way they looked at each other, how comfortable they seemed together. "Congratulations, I guess. If you're happy."

"I am," she said, her expression softening. "Very happy."

A silence stretched between them. He realized she was waiting for more from him—approval, perhaps, or enthusiasm.

"Jonah seems like a good man," he offered.

"He is." Her eyes held his. "I wanted to tell you first, before anyone else. We'll announce it to others in a few days."

He was strangely touched by that. For years, he'd felt like an afterthought in his mother's life, someone she'd given up trying to understand. Yet here she was, sharing her news with him first.

"Thank you for telling me," he said.

"I never thought I'd marry again…" She trailed off, looking down at her hands.

"Mother, you deserve someone who treats you like you deserve to be treated. I'm sorry I wasn't on board with Jonah at first, but that's because I didn't really know him." He shrugged. "You deserve to be happy."

She looked up, surprise flickering across her face. "You think so?"

"Of course I do. Why wouldn't I?"

She hesitated. "I thought perhaps you might disapprove. Think I was being… foolish at my age."

He shook his head. "Not at all."

"Or that I was betraying your father's memory somehow."

He couldn't help the short snorting laugh that escaped him. "I think Dad forfeited any right to that kind of loyalty a long time ago." The words came out more bitter than he intended.

She looked at him sharply. "What do you mean by that?"

He sighed. "Nothing. No, it's not nothing." He ran a hand through his hair. "Dad wasn't exactly the model husband, was he? The late nights, the business trips that seemed to go on longer than they should have."

Her face lost some of its color. "You knew about that?"

"I wasn't blind, Mother. Or deaf. I heard the arguments."

She looked away. "I never wanted you to know."

"Kids pick up on more than parents think." He leaned forward in his chair. "Look, I'm happy for you. Really. Jonah seems to treat you well. Better than Dad ever did."

"Your father wasn't always…" She stopped, seeming to reconsider her words. "Theodore had his failings, but he provided for us."

"Is that enough? Just providing?" He hadn't meant to get into this, but now that they were talking about his father, the words kept coming. "He made you miserable half the time. Made me feel like I could never measure up."

She looked at him in silence for a long moment. "I know things weren't always good between you and your father. I should have done more. Should have seen how much his words hurt you."

The simple acknowledgment felt like the lifting of a weight he had carried for decades. "I spent years trying to prove him wrong. That I wasn't worthless, that I could amount to something."

"Is that why you're so determined to build this development? To prove something?"

He hesitated. Was she right? Was this project just another attempt to show his father—even in death—that he was successful? That he mattered?

"Maybe partly," he admitted. "But I also genuinely believe it would be good for Magnolia Key. The town needs to grow, to have a stable economic future."

His mother nodded slowly. "I'm beginning to understand that you see it that way. I don't agree with the specific plan, but I believe you when you say your intentions aren't purely selfish."

Coming from his mother, this was practically a full endorsement. He felt something loosen in his chest. "Thank you for that."

They sat in silence for a moment, the conversation having taken them places neither had expected to go.

"So," he said finally. "You and Jonah. When's the wedding?"

A small smile touched her lips. "We haven't set a date yet. Something small, I think. Nothing elaborate. And fairly soon. We've waited a long time for it."

"Makes sense." He paused. "Does he make you laugh?"

The question seemed to surprise her. "Yes, he does. Quite often, actually."

"Good. You rarely laughed when I was growing up."

Her eyes softened. "Perhaps I didn't."

He stood up. "Well, I should get going. I promised Tori I'd help at the theater this morning."

His mother rose as well. "You've been doing a lot to help people after the storm."

"Just trying to be useful."

"It hasn't gone unnoticed." She hesitated, then added, "I'm proud of you for that, Cliff."

The words stunned him. When was the last time his mother had said she was proud of him? Had she ever?

"Thanks," he managed. "That… means a lot."

"Perhaps we could have dinner together tonight? You, me, and Jonah? To celebrate."

He nodded. "I'd like that."

As he headed out the door a few minutes later, he found himself smiling. His mother was getting married. And she was proud of him. Two things he never thought he'd see happen.

The morning sun felt warm on his face as he walked toward Coastal Coffee. He considered skipping breakfast and heading right to the theater since it was later than he'd hoped to start this morning. And truly, he needed time to process this conversation with his mother—the most honest one they'd had in years.

But then, he couldn't bear not seeing Beverly.

So many changes in his life.

But maybe things really were changing in Magnolia Key. And maybe, just maybe, those changes would be for the better.

A week later, Beverly cleared a table at Coastal Coffee as the breakfast crowd was winding down. Business had picked back up since the hurricane, and she was grateful for it. The town was healing, rebuilding, and moving forward.

The bell over the door jingled, and she looked up to see Cliff entering. He wore a casual button-down shirt with the sleeves rolled up to his elbows. His hair was slightly tousled, likely from the ocean breeze that had picked up this morning.

"Morning," he called out as he approached the counter.

"Morning." Ignoring what just the glimpse of him did to her heart, she grabbed a coffee mug and poured him his usual. "Just missed the rush."

"That was deliberate." His mouth quirked into a

half-smile. "Hoping you'd have time to take a break with me."

She handed him the steaming mug. "And your timing is impeccable. I was hoping to take a break."

They headed over to a quiet corner and sat at a table. She leaned forward on the table, watching him. "So, I heard the big news."

"About my mother and Jonah? Hard to miss it." He chuckled. "I think Mrs. Henderson stopped me in the street just mere moments after my mother told me."

She smiled. "News travels fast on Magnolia Key."

"You don't say." The dry humor in his voice made her laugh.

"How do you feel about it?" she asked, genuinely curious. He had a such a complicated relationship with his mother and father.

He ran his finger around the rim of his coffee cup, considering his answer. "I'm happy for her. Jonah is a great guy, and I hope they'll be very happy together." He looked up, meeting her eyes directly. "Everyone deserves a second chance."

The pointed look he gave her wasn't subtle. A warm flush crept up her neck, and she busied herself straightening the salt and pepper shaker on the table.

"I suppose they do," she finally said, not quite meeting his gaze.

"The town's certainly buzzing about it," he continued. "I've never seen my mother the subject of so much speculation and attention. She's actually enjoying it, though she'd never admit it."

She smiled, thinking of how Eleanor had come in yesterday, pretending to be annoyed by all the well-wishers but practically glowing with happiness.

"She seems different. Softer somehow."

"Love will do that to a person." He took another sip of his coffee. "Even to someone as formidable as Eleanor Griffin."

"I never thought I'd see the day when Eleanor would be beaming like a schoolgirl in love," she said, remembering how Eleanor and Jonah had sat at their usual table yesterday morning, heads bent together, whispering and laughing. "I think… well, I think I heard your mother… giggle."

"Giggle? My mother?" His eyebrows shot up. "Now that I would pay good money to see."

"Well, as close to giggling as Eleanor gets," she amended with a smile. "It was more like… restrained amusement with the occasional uncharacteristic laugh."

"Still sounds like a miracle to me." He took a sip of his coffee and set the mug down. "And you know what? She made a point to tell me first, before anyone else found out."

She could see how that moved him. She reached over and placed her hand over his. "I'm glad. It really seems like you and your mother are working things out."

"I think so." He shrugged. "At least we're trying."

"When's the wedding?"

"Next month, from what I hear. Small ceremony at the gazebo on the beach and a reception at Mother's house. Nothing fancy, believe it or not. Doesn't sound like a wedding I'd ever imagined for my mother."

"Good for her for doing exactly what she wants."

"She said she didn't want to wait—at their age, they don't have time to waste." He shook his head. "Never thought I'd hear my mother talk like that."

"She's embracing life. It's nice to see."

The cafe was empty now except for the two of them. Through the front windows, she could see people walking along the street, stopping to chat with neighbors. Life on Magnolia Key was returning to normal, or as normal as it could be with half the bridge still out and repairs ongoing throughout the island.

"Any word on when they'll start rebuilding the bridge?" she asked, changing the subject.

"County is looking into it, but you know how these things go. Could be six months… could be never. There's talk of permanently adding a second ferry."

"A second ferry would be nice."

"That's what Magnolia Key does," he said. "Adapts and survives."

She nodded. They sat in comfortable silence for a moment. She realized how strange it was that she could now be comfortable in silence with Cliff when just a few weeks ago she'd wanted nothing more than for him to leave town and never come back.

"Beverly," he said suddenly, "I was wondering if you'd like to have dinner with me tonight? To discuss another fundraiser," he added quickly.

Another fundraiser. The first one last weekend had been a great success, and she mentioned in passing about organizing another one for the hurricane relief fund, but they hadn't made any concrete plans yet.

"Sure," she said before she could overthink it. "That would be nice."

"Great." His smile was warm. "I'll pick you up at six?"

"Six works." She tried to ignore the flutter in her stomach. This wasn't a date. It was a planning meeting for a community fundraiser. That's all.

"Looking forward to it." He placed a few bills on the table, more than enough for the coffee. "Keep the change."

"You don't have to—"

"I want to," he insisted. "Every little bit helps, right?"

She nodded, unable to argue with that logic. "See you tonight."

As he headed for the door, the bell jingled again, and Maxine walked in.

"Morning," Maxine called out cheerfully, then noticed Cliff. "Oh, hello, Cliff."

"Maxine," he nodded. "Good to see you. I was just heading out."

After he left, Maxine raised an eyebrow. "Just another late breakfast together?"

"It was nothing," she said too quickly, and Maxine stared at her for a moment. "We were just talking about Eleanor and Jonah's engagement."

"Uh-huh." Her friend didn't look convinced. "And that's why your cheeks are pink?"

"My cheeks are not pink." She touched her face self-consciously.

"If you say so." Maxine grinned. "So, what's the latest on the engagement? I heard Miss Eleanor actually let Darlene take her shopping for a dress in Sarasota yesterday."

"Really?" She couldn't imagine Eleanor being willing to make a fuss over a wedding dress, although she was always impeccably dressed.

"Told Darlene she didn't want anything fancy, but you know Darlene." Maxine chuckled. "I'm betting Eleanor comes back with something a lot fancier than she intended."

"Good for her. She deserves to feel special."

"Speaking of special." Maxine gave her a hard look. "What's going on with you and Cliff? And don't say nothing because I've known you too long to fall for that."

She sighed, knowing Maxine wouldn't let it go. "We're having dinner tonight."

"A date?" Maxine's eyes gleamed.

"No, not a date. We're planning another fundraiser for the hurricane relief fund."

"Sure, a 'fundraiser.'" Maxine made air quotes. "Just the two of you, having dinner, planning a 'fundraiser.'"

"It's not like that." But even as she said it, she wasn't entirely sure that was the truth.

"Keep telling yourself that," Maxine said with a knowing smile. "You know, it's okay to admit you still have feelings for him."

"I don't…" She stopped. What was the point in denying it? "I don't know what I feel, Maxine. Some days, I still remember how hurt I was when he left. Other days…"

"Other days, you see the man he's become," Maxine finished for her. "And now you know the truth about why he left."

She nodded. "It's complicated."

"Life usually is." Maxine squeezed her hand. "Just be open to possibilities, okay? Like you said, Eleanor is embracing life. Maybe you should too."

~

Beverly stood in front of her closet, examining the contents with a critical eye. What did one wear to a dinner that wasn't a date but somehow felt like one? She pushed hangers aside, rejecting outfit after outfit. The blue sundress was too casual. The black dress too formal. The white blouse with slacks too businesslike.

"This is ridiculous," she muttered to herself. "It's just dinner to discuss a fundraiser."

She glanced at the clock. Five-thirty already. Cliff would be here in half an hour, and she was still in her bathrobe with wet hair from her shower. She pulled out a simple teal dress she hadn't worn in ages. It had short sleeves and a modest V-neck that highlighted her collarbone without being too revealing. The fabric fell just below her knees, flattering her figure without clinging too tightly.

"This will do," she decided, laying it on the bed. She quickly blow-dried her hair, letting it fall in loose waves around her shoulders instead of pulling it back as usual.

As she applied a subtle layer of makeup—more than her usual workday routine but not too much— she questioned her own motives. Why was she putting in this extra effort? This wasn't a date. It was two community-minded people discussing a fundraiser.

Yet her hands trembled slightly as she fastened small silver earrings and spritzed on a light perfume she rarely wore.

"Get a grip, Beverly," she told her reflection. "You're acting like a teenager."

The dress slipped on easily, and she paired it with comfortable but nice sandals. No point in torturing herself with heels on Magnolia Key's cobblestone streets. She was just fastening her favorite silver bracelet around her wrist when a knock sounded at the door.

Her heart jumped. She glanced at the clock—five minutes to six. Cliff was early. She took a deep breath, smoothed her dress, and made her way to the door.

When she opened it, the sight of him momentarily stole her breath away. He stood on her porch in dark slacks and a light blue button-down shirt that matched his eyes perfectly. His hair was neatly combed, and he'd shaved since this morning.

"Hi," she said, hating how breathless she sounded.

"Hi." His eyes swept over her, appreciation evident in his gaze. "You look beautiful."

"Thank you." Heat crept up her neck. "You clean up pretty well yourself."

He smiled, and she noticed he was holding something behind his back. "These are for you," he said, revealing a small bouquet of flowers. "I stole them from Jonah's garden." He grinned. "Just kidding. Jonah suggested I pick some."

"They're lovely," she said, taking them. The casual gesture somehow meant more than a formal bouquet would have. "Let me put them in water before we go."

She retreated to the kitchen, grateful for a moment to collect herself. Her heart was fluttering, and her pulse was rampaging through her. "Get a grip, Beverly," she told herself again. As she arranged the flowers in a small vase, she reminded herself once more that this was not a date. The flowers didn't mean anything. They were just being friendly.

When she returned, Cliff was standing in her living room, looking at the framed photos on her mantel. A photo from the first day she opened Coastal Coffee. A few photos of her and Maxine through the years. What wasn't there was a photo of her and Cliff.

"Ready?" she asked.

He turned and nodded. "Shall we?"

The evening air was perfect as they stepped outside—warm but not humid, with a gentle breeze coming off the water. She locked her door, and they set off down the street toward the boardwalk.

"I thought we'd go to Sharky's, if that's okay with you," he said. "Unless you had somewhere else in mind."

"Sharky's is perfect." It was casual enough not to feel too date-like but nice enough for an evening out.

They walked side by side, close but not touching. The silence between them wasn't uncomfortable, but she felt a nervous energy that made her want to fill it.

"Do you have any ideas about this second fundraiser?" he finally asked.

She began to relax. This was familiar territory—planning, organizing, helping the community. The nervous flutter in her stomach subsided somewhat as they approached the boardwalk.

"I do. I've made a list."

"Of course you have." He grinned at her.

They continued down the boardwalk to Sharky's. The restaurant was busy but not packed. The hostess led them to a table near the windows with a view of the water. The sun was beginning its descent, painting the sky in shades of pink and orange.

"This is nice," she said as they settled into their chairs.

"It is." But his eyes were on her rather than the view.

They ordered drinks—a glass of white wine for her, a beer for him—and studied the menus. She was acutely aware of the glances from other diners. Mrs. Peterson and her husband were at a table near the bar, and she caught the older woman watching them with unabashed interest.

Cliff must have noticed too. "I think we're providing the evening's entertainment," he said with a wry smile.

She grimaced. "We're sure to be as big a subject of gossip as your mother's impending wedding. By tomorrow morning, half the town will have heard we were here together."

They ordered dinner and talked about another fundraiser. "This one will need to be different. Maybe we can think of something that will even attract people from the mainland." She frowned, trying to come up with an original idea.

"Especially if that second ferry starts running."

She frowned for a moment. "If they don't get funding to continue the bridge… are you still going ahead with your development plans?"

She studied Cliff's face as she waited for his answer. The gentle clinking of silverware and murmured conversations of other diners faded into the background as she focused on him. The sun continued to lower toward the horizon outside the windows, casting a golden glow across the water.

He took a sip of his beer, then set it down with a deliberate motion. "Yes," he said finally. "I am going ahead with my plans. The island needs this development. The hurricane only proves it more.

There are businesses that barely survived the storm. We need to diversify the economy here."

She felt like a cold, hard stone settled in her chest. Despite their recent reconnection, some things hadn't changed.

"Even with the bridge delayed?"

"The bridge will get built eventually. It's just a matter of time and funding." He nodded confidently. "And when it does, Magnolia Key needs to be ready. This development will bring jobs, tax revenue, and tourists who will spend money at local businesses."

Including Coastal Coffee, she thought. Yet the idea still troubled her.

"What about the height variance? Are you still pushing for six stories?"

"I need at least five to make the numbers work," he said, his expression turning more businesslike. "Four would be a stretch financially."

Their server arrived with their meals—grilled grouper for her, steak for him. She waited until they were alone again before continuing.

"Don't you want Magnolia Key to stay like it is?" she asked, setting her fork down without taking a bite. "A quaint little town where people know each other and come together in times of crisis? Like they did after the hurricane."

His eyes met hers, and she saw frustration there,

but also something else—a need to make her understand.

"Of course I do," he said. "I love this island. I always have."

"Then why change it?" She gestured toward the window. "Look at this view. Look at how everyone in this restaurant knows everyone else. This is special. This is what makes Magnolia Key what it is."

He sighed. "Places change, Beverly. They have to. If they don't grow, they die."

"Growth doesn't have to mean high-rise buildings blocking the view of the water," she countered.

"No, but it does mean progress. Development. New opportunities. Jobs." He leaned forward. "The younger generation is leaving, Beverly. They're going to the mainland for jobs, for better opportunities. We need to give them reasons to stay."

She hadn't thought about it that way. "But at what cost?"

"That's what we need to figure out. There has to be a balance."

She took a small bite of her fish, chewing slowly as she considered his words. When she looked up, she found Cliff watching her.

"You know," she said softly, "you don't have to prove anything to anyone…"

His expression shifted, a flash of something vulnerable crossing his features before he masked it.

"…except maybe to yourself," she finished.

He stared at her, his fork suspended in midair. "What do you mean?" His voice was quiet, careful.

She set down her own fork and reached for her wineglass, taking a small sip before answering. "Now that I know what happened with your father and how he treated you…" She hesitated, then decided to push forward. "Are you sure this development isn't about proving him wrong? Showing that you can succeed where he said you'd fail?"

His jaw tightened. He set his fork down with a controlled movement that betrayed the tension in his hand. "This isn't about my father."

"Isn't it?" she asked gently. "At least a little bit?"

He looked away, his gaze finding the darkening water outside. "Maybe it was at first," he admitted after a long moment. "When I first started planning it. I wanted to show him what I could do. Show the town. But now… now it's about more than that."

"What is it about now?"

"It's about building something that matters. Something that lasts." He turned back to her. "And yes, maybe part of me still wants to prove that I can do something meaningful. Not just to my father's ghost, but to myself. Is that so wrong?"

"No," she said finally. "It's not wrong to want to build something meaningful. But does it have to be this particular development? In this particular place?"

"I've put a lot of work into this project," he said. "Years of planning."

"I understand that." She paused. "But after everything that's happened—the hurricane, seeing how the community came together—are you sure this is still what Magnolia Key needs?"

A shadow of doubt crossed his face, so briefly she might have imagined it. "I believe it is."

They ate in silence for a few moments. She searched for the right words, wanting to make him see her perspective without pushing him away again.

"The night of the town council meeting," she began, "you said something about bringing Magnolia Key into the future."

"I remember."

"But what if the future of Magnolia isn't about big developments and high-rise buildings? What if it's about preserving what makes this place special while still allowing for growth?"

He frowned slightly. "What are you suggesting?"

"I don't know exactly," she admitted. "But maybe there's a way to develop that property that honors the character of the island. Something that adds to what we have without fundamentally changing it."

Cliff took another bite of his steak, chewing thoughtfully. "Like what?"

She grinned at him. "I'm not sure. You're the big-shot developer."

Their server returned to check on them, momentarily interrupting their conversation. When she left, Cliff studied Beverly with a thoughtful expression.

"You really care about this place, don't you?" he asked.

"It's my home. It's where I belong."

Something shifted in his gaze. "It was my home too, once."

"It could be again… If you wanted it to be."

The implication of her words hung between them, layered with meaning that went beyond the development project.

He set his napkin down beside his plate. "I'll think about what you've said. About a different approach to the development."

"That's all I'm asking," she said, relief washing through her. It wasn't a promise to change his plans, but it was an opening. A willingness to consider alternatives.

They turned the conversation to lighter topics as they finished their meal—the upcoming fundraiser they'd originally planned to discuss, Eleanor and Jonah's engagement, and the progress of repairs around the island. By the time they declined dessert and asked for the check, the tension had eased.

Outside, the sky had darkened, but the boardwalk was lit by the warm glow of streetlamps. They walked slowly, in no hurry to end the evening.

"Thank you for dinner." She paused as they neared the end of the boardwalk.

"Thank you for the company. And for the perspective. You always did have a way of making me… listen."

"Except that time I told you not to take your father's car, and it ended up in the bay, didn't it?" She bumped her shoulder into his, smiling.

He laughed. "Okay, I really should have listened to you that time."

They continued on their way until they reached her cottage. They stood on her porch steps with the stars twinkling above them. He took her hand in his, his grip firm and his skin roughened from the manual work he'd been doing. He looked straight into her eyes. "I do enjoy spending time with you. You're the one person I feel like I can be myself with… and you'll accept me."

She reached out and touched his face. "You're a good man, Cliff Griffin."

He covered her hand with his own. "I've spent so long trying to prove myself…"

"You don't have to prove anything to me."

The words hung in the air between them as she

gazed up at him. His hand still covered hers against his cheek, warm and solid. Her heartbeat quickened as his eyes darkened, moving from her eyes to her lips and back again. The gentle breeze rustled the leaves of the magnolia tree beside her porch, and somewhere in the distance, she could hear the faint sound of music drifting from the boardwalk.

Time seemed to slow as Cliff leaned toward her, his intention clear in his eyes. She had a fleeting moment to decide—to step back or to stay. She stayed, her feet planted on the wooden porch as if they belonged there.

And then his lips found hers.

The kiss was gentle at first, almost questioning, as if he expected her to pull away. But she didn't want to pull away. Instead, she leaned into him, her hand sliding from his cheek to the back of his neck. His arms wrapped around her waist, drawing her closer.

It had been so long—decades—since they'd kissed. The last time, they'd been two teenagers with their whole lives ahead of them, standing on the beach with stars overhead, making promises they couldn't keep. Now they were adults with years of living behind them, standing on her porch with those same stars watching.

Yet something about this felt both new and familiar at once. His lips were softer than she remembered, but they moved against hers with the same sureness, the same perfect rhythm they'd found all those years ago.

She closed her eyes as she surrendered to the moment. The years between their last kiss and this one seemed to fall away. All the hurt, all the misunderstandings, all the loneliness—none of it mattered in this perfect moment where there was only Cliff and the feel of his arms around her.

She'd kissed other men in the years since Cliff— but nothing had ever felt quite like this. It was as if a piece of herself that had been missing for years had suddenly fallen back into place. A warm sense of rightness flooded through her, and she found herself smiling even as they continued to kiss.

Cliff must have felt her smile because he pulled back slightly, his eyes searching hers. His own lips curved upward in response. The look in his eyes— tender, questioning, hopeful—made her heart skip a beat.

"Beverly," he whispered, his voice husky.

She reached up to touch his face again, tracing the line of his jaw with her fingertips. "That was…" She paused, searching for the right word.

"Long overdue?" he offered, his smile widening.

She laughed softly. "Yes. That."

He took her hands in his, interlacing their fingers. "I've wanted to do that since the moment I saw you again."

"Even when I was glaring at you across the town hall?"

"Even then," he admitted. "Maybe especially then. You were always beautiful when you were passionate about something."

She blushed, feeling suddenly shy despite the fact that they'd just been kissing like teenagers. "I don't know what happens next," she confessed.

"Neither do I," he said. "But I'd like to find out. If you would."

She looked at their joined hands, then back up at his face—the face she'd once known better than her own, now lined with years of experiences she knew nothing about. Years they could have shared if things had been different. But they weren't different. They were here now, two people with complicated histories finding their way back to each other.

"I would. I'd like to find out too."

He smiled then, a real smile that reached his eyes and made them crinkle at the corners. He leaned forward and pressed his forehead against hers, their breath mingling in the small space between them.

"Good," he whispered. "You have no idea how much I've missed you."

And yet, she knew exactly how much, because she'd missed him that much and maybe more.

CHAPTER 25

Cliff came in every morning for breakfast, and Beverly couldn't help the automatic smile that came to her lips every time he walked through the door… or the flutter in her heart. But in spite of the joy in her heart, it had been a rough week. A town meeting had been called about Cliff's project. And it didn't help that Maxine and Dale were on vacation together, so she didn't have her best friend to talk to.

Beverly flipped the sign to open at Coastal Coffee, inhaling the rich aroma of freshly ground beans that wafted across the cafe. Sunlight was just beginning to light the sky out the window. Although the pink sky of sunrise promised the beginning of a nice day, a heaviness hung over her.

The town meeting about Cliff's development

project was scheduled for tonight, and she'd watched the tension building all week. The hurricane recovery had brought Magnolia Key together in a beautiful way, with neighbors helping neighbors and differences set aside for the common good. But as repairs progressed and life started to return to normal, the divisions were resurfacing, deeper than before.

She arranged pastries in the display case, trying to ignore the knot in her stomach. Her feelings for Cliff had grown stronger since their kiss, but their relationship existed in a strange limbo. How could she fall for someone whose vision for Magnolia Key threatened to change everything she loved about her home?

The bell above the door jingled as her first customers arrived. "Morning, Nash," she called out as he took a table.

As the usual morning crowd of locals stopped in before work, she greeted them with a practiced smile, pouring coffee and making small talk as she had thousands of times before. But today, she noticed the subtle divisions. People clustered at different tables and conversations hushed when certain folks walked by.

Mrs. Peterson leaned over the counter as Beverly refilled her cup. "You'll be at the meeting tonight, won't you? We need sensible voices to speak up against that monstrosity."

Before she could answer, Tim Marshall called from his nearby table. "That so-called monstrosity will bring jobs we desperately need, especially after the hurricane. Some people just can't see past their own front porches."

Mrs. Peterson's face reddened. "Some people would sell their grandmother for a dollar."

"No one's selling anything," she said softly, trying to defuse the tension. "The council just wants to hear everyone's thoughts."

But her words went unheard as Tim pushed back his chair and approached the counter, coffee mug in hand. "The bridge is gone. Tourism is down. What's your plan for keeping this town alive? More bake sales?"

She set down the coffeepot. "Tim, please. Can we just—"

"It's not about jobs," Mrs. Peterson interrupted. "It's about protecting what makes this place special. Once those big buildings go up, we can't go back."

Tim scoffed. "Special won't pay the bills when half the businesses close."

Her chest tightened as she watched the exchange. These were people who'd been friends for decades, who'd helped each other clear debris after the hurricane just weeks ago. Now, they could barely speak civilly. Tim turned and stalked back to his table.

Other customers joined in, voices rising around

the cafe. She moved between tables, refilling cups and trying to maintain peace, but the arguments only intensified.

"That Griffin boy never cared about this town," someone called out. "Just another developer looking to make a buck."

"That *boy* stayed behind during the hurricane and has been helping rebuild ever since," another countered.

She turned around, coffeepot in hand, as heated voices erupted from a table by the window. Sarah Smith and Greg Wark were nearly nose to nose, faces flushed with anger.

"You're being selfish!" Sarah snapped. "Not everyone has a trust fund to fall back on."

"And you're being shortsighted!" Greg shot back. "This is about our children's future too!"

She started toward them, determined to intervene before things escalated further, when movement at the door caught her eye. The bell jangled loudly as someone burst in, and to her complete surprise, she saw Maxine rush into the cafe, looking windblown and slightly frazzled.

She stopped in her tracks. "What are you doing here? You're not supposed to be back for two more days."

Maxine weaved through the tables, ignoring the ongoing arguments. "We decided we needed to be back for tonight's town meeting. It's important."

She wrapped Beverly in a fierce hug, and the familiar scent of her friend's perfume momentarily drowned out the tension in the room. She clung to her, suddenly realizing how much she'd needed her friend's presence.

"Thank goodness you're here," she whispered. "It's getting nasty."

Maxine pulled back, glancing around at the heated conversations still bouncing off the walls of the cafe. "So I see. Dale will be here in a minute. He's parking the car."

"Coffee?" Beverly asked, already reaching for a clean mug.

"Please. Strong enough to stand a spoon in it." Maxine slid onto a stool at the counter, dropping her purse beside her. "Drove all night to get back."

She poured her a cup. "You didn't have to cut your vacation short."

"Of course we did. This is our town too. And I wasn't about to let you face this alone."

The cafe door opened again as Dale entered, looking travel-weary. He gave her a quick wave before stopping to break up Sarah and Greg's increasingly loud argument.

"Has it been like this all week?" Maxine asked, lowering her voice.

She nodded, leaning against the counter. "It started small. It was just comments here and there. But it's getting worse. People who've been neighbors for decades suddenly can't stand each other."

"And Cliff?" Maxine raised an eyebrow.

Her cheeks grew warm. "He still comes in for breakfast, but I haven't seen him much besides that. He's been really busy. Getting ready for tonight's meeting, I guess. But we're careful not to discuss the development when we're together."

"That doesn't sound… sustainable."

"It's not," she admitted. "But I don't know what else to do. I care about him, Maxine. More than I thought possible. But I also care about Magnolia Key staying Magnolia Key."

A crash from across the room made them both jump. Someone had knocked over a chair while gesturing emphatically.

"Enough!" she called out, louder than she'd intended. The cafe fell silent, all eyes turning toward her. "This is still my coffee shop, and I won't have neighbors treating each other this way. Save it for the meeting tonight."

People shuffled awkwardly, murmuring apologies as they returned to their seats or gathered their belongings to leave. She took a deep breath, surprised by her own outburst.

"Well done." Maxine smiled with approval.

She shook her head. "I hate this, Max. It feels like the hurricane brought us together, and now Cliff's project is tearing us apart again."

"People are scared. Change is always frightening, especially when it's happening to something you love."

"I know. And that's what makes this so hard." She absently wiped the counter. "Part of me understands Cliff's vision. The bridge is gone, tourism will suffer, and businesses are struggling. But another part of me loves this island exactly as it is."

"And you're caught in the middle."

She nodded, feeling trapped. "I keep thinking about what Eleanor said about her great-aunt Vera and how she chose love over what was expected of her. But this isn't just about Cliff and me. It's about the future of our whole community."

Dale approached the counter, having successfully calmed Sarah and Greg. "If those two are any indication, tonight's meeting is going to be a doozy."

"That's what I'm afraid of," she said.

Dale's eyes were twinkling, though, as he draped an arm around Maxine's shoulders. "Did you tell her?"

"Not yet. I was waiting for you."

"Tell me what?" She eyed them suspiciously.

"This." Maxine held her hand up with a flourish. "We're engaged! Dale asked me to marry him."

She hurried around the counter and threw her arms around her friend. "Oh, Maxine, I'm so happy for you." She pulled back and grinned at Dale. "You got yourself a good one."

"Don't I know it." Dale beamed.

Her heart was happy for her friend. Maxine deserved this and so much more. At least there was one bright spot in this turbulent day.

Beverly walked into the town hall with her stomach in knots. The space was already packed with agitated locals, their voices a mix of heated debate and terse whispers. She squeezed past several neighbors, nodding politely but avoiding getting pulled into any discussions. Not yet. Not until she'd sorted out her own tangled thoughts.

She spotted Maxine and Dale across the room, saving her a seat. But before she could reach them, Cliff appeared at her side, his face tight with tension despite his attempt at an easy smile. There was no fancy suit this time. He was dressed in jeans and a button-down shirt with the sleeves rolled up slightly.

"Hey," he said softly, taking her hand and giving it a gentle squeeze. "It will be okay."

She looked up into his eyes, searching for certainty she couldn't find in herself. "Will it?"

"Trust me," he replied, his voice low and intimate despite the crowd surrounding them.

She wanted to believe him. Over the past weeks, she'd come to understand why this project mattered so much to Cliff. It wasn't just business. It was personal validation. A chance to prove to everyone in Magnolia Key, especially his mother, that he wasn't the failure Theodore had labeled him. That he could be successful on his own terms. That he belonged.

But understanding his motivation didn't change her conviction that his high-rise would forever alter the character of their island. The very essence of what made Magnolia Key special would be compromised.

"I should find my seat," she said, reluctantly pulling her hand from his. "They're about to start."

He nodded, disappointment flickering across his features. "We'll talk after?"

"Of course," she promised, though she wondered if they'd have anything left to say when this was over.

She made her way to Maxine, who immediately sensed her distress.

"You okay?" Maxine whispered as Beverly slid into the wooden chair beside her.

"Not really," she admitted, taking in the room. The town had physically divided itself—those supporting the development clustered on the right side of the hall, those opposing it gathered on the left. A vivid visual of the rift in their community.

The mayor called the meeting to order, his gavel barely audible over the murmurs of the crowd. "Folks, as you know, we're here tonight to discuss the proposed development at the end of the boardwalk. The planning commission wants to hear more comments from the community before making their decision. They realize this is an important decision to make."

She spotted Eleanor and Jonah sitting near the front, Eleanor's back ramrod straight. At least Eleanor and Cliff were speaking now, though she suspected tonight might test their fragile reconciliation.

Cliff rose from his seat on the stage, but the mayor held up his hand. "We've all heard Mr. Griffin's plans, so we'll start with comments from the audience."

The mayor's gaze swept across the packed town hall as he motioned toward the microphone up front. Her heart hammered against her ribs. She'd spent the entire day rehearsing what she would say, knowing her words could drive a permanent wedge between her and Cliff. But she couldn't stay silent, not when the future of Magnolia Key hung in the balance.

Before anyone else could move, she rose to her feet. Maxine reached up and squeezed her hand.

"You sure?" Maxine whispered.

She nodded, her throat tight. If she didn't speak now, she might lose her nerve entirely.

She made her way to the center aisle, feeling dozens of stares focused on her. Familiar faces watched her—some hopeful, some wary. She spotted Mrs. Henderson, who'd been bringing her grandchildren to Coastal Coffee every Saturday for years. Patty Miller, whose roof Cliff had personally helped repair after the hurricane. Each person represented a different part of the community she loved, a community that was being torn apart by this decision.

As she approached the microphone, she felt like she was being pulled in two directions. She understood Cliff's need to prove himself, to build something meaningful. But she also knew what made their island special, and it wasn't luxury high-rises.

The wooden floorboards creaked under her feet as she stepped up front. As she adjusted the microphone, the feedback caused a momentary screech that silenced the room.

"My name is Beverly Mooney," she began, her voice steadier than she felt. "I've lived on Magnolia Key my entire life. Coastal Coffee has been my business for over twenty years now, and I've seen a lot of changes in our town during that time."

She paused, gathering her thoughts. From the

corner of her eye, she saw Cliff sitting at the side of the stage with the planning commission members. She ignored him. Or tried to.

"I understand the appeal of progress and development. But I believe this particular project would fundamentally alter what makes our island special. The height alone would change our skyline forever. And while jobs are important, we need to ask ourselves what kind of community we want to—"

Movement from the stage interrupted her. Cliff had risen from his seat and was approaching the microphone.

"Please," he said, his voice carrying through the room without the need for amplification. "If I could say a word first."

She stepped back, startled. This wasn't part of the normal procedure for these meetings. She glanced at the mayor, who seemed equally surprised but gave a small nod of acquiescence.

Cliff moved to stand beside her at the microphone. Up close, she could see the tension in his jaw and the crease between his brows. But there was something else in his eyes. There was a certainty she hadn't seen before.

"I apologize for interrupting," he said, addressing both Beverly and the crowd. "But before anyone speaks for or against the original proposal, I'd like everyone to see something important."

She stepped back to give him the microphone, annoyed he was interrupting her.

"I know many of you have concerns about the changes my development might bring to Magnolia Key. I understand those concerns. This island has been my home too. It shaped me, even during the years I was away."

She tensed, waiting for his usual speech about economic benefits, tax revenue, and job creation. She'd heard it all before and had prepared her own counterarguments, mentally rehearsing what she would say when it was her turn to speak. She grew more annoyed that he'd interrupted her. She wanted to state again how she was against the project, against Cliff, despite their personal relationship. How she knew she would choose the island over love. It was that important to her.

But something in Cliff's manner made her pause. He seemed different tonight—less defensive, more thoughtful as he looked around the room, meeting the eyes of his neighbors and former classmates.

"The hurricane changed things for all of us," he said, his gaze finding hers. "It reminded me what matters most about this place. We all came together to rebuild after the hurricane, and a very smart woman helped me see that's what's important. It's not the buildings or the boardwalk. It's the people. The community."

She couldn't take her eyes from him, and a flicker of hope kindled deep inside of her.

"I now more fully understand the concerns about preserving Magnolia Key's character," he said. "That's why we've made several modifications to the original plans."

He gestured to one of his assistants, who quickly placed mounted boards with on the easels on the stage. These showed a different building than he'd presented before. Instead of the modern high-rise, these showed what could only be called quintessential old Florida, with architectural elements that echoed the island's historical structures.

"We were able to buy the adjoining lot to the one we previously purchased. We have redesigned the facade to incorporate traditional materials. The ground floor will feature covered walkways with arches similar to those on the town hall and the library. And you'll see…" He paused and looked at her again. "It will now be only two stories tall. Shops and restaurants on the lower level, and condos on the second story, keeping within Magnolia's current building codes."

A gasp ran through the crowd, and many of the council members leaned forward, studying the drawings with interest.

"Additionally, we're creating a dedicated space in the lobby for a permanent historical exhibit about the boardwalk and early Magnolia Key. I'm working with the historical society to ensure the display properly honors the island's heritage."

A ripple of low comments ran through the hall.

"As for the environmental concerns," he continued, "we've partnered with marine scientists to ensure minimal impact on the shoreline. And while the building's footprint is larger since we spread out between the two lots, the overall size of the building is smaller since we lowered the height."

He pointed to another board showing detailed diagrams. "We've also incorporated green building practices throughout the design. Solar panels, rainwater collection systems, and native landscaping will make this one of the most environmentally sustainable buildings on the coast."

She felt her own certainty waver as she studied the new plans. The modified design was beautiful, she had to admit. It managed to echo the past while looking toward the future. Several council members were exchanging approving glances.

"But most importantly," Cliff said, his voice softening slightly, "we're preserving public access to the waterfront. The boardwalk will be widened, with new seating areas where families can still gather to watch those sunsets we all love."

Applause rang through the town hall as people jumped to their feet. After a few minutes, the mayor banged his gravel again, a wide grin on his face.

"With no variance needed on our regular building codes, I guess this meeting is adjourned. Mr. Griffin, we look forward to working with you."

She stepped to the side as many of the townsfolk came forward to shake Cliff's hand. Maxine walked up beside her. "Well, that was surprising."

"It was, wasn't it?"

"Did you know he'd changed all his plans?"

"No, he didn't say a word. I guess this is what he was so busy working on this week."

Eleanor and Jonah joined them. "Well, I must say, Cliff surprised me with all this." Eleanor looked over to where Cliff stood surrounded by people congratulating him, smiles on their faces.

As the crowd thinned, Cliff made his way over to where they all were standing. Eleanor beamed at her son. "You made me proud, son."

"Well, you were right, Mother."

"What? I'm not sure I heard you correctly." Eleanor's lips rose into a grin.

"You were right."

"Ah, the words every mother longs to hear from her son."

They all laughed, and Eleanor took Jonah's hand. "We should leave. I believe that my son and Beverly have some things to discuss."

"Yes, ma'am, Ellie." Jonah's eyes shone with love for Eleanor.

Dale wrapped his arm around Maxine's waist,

and her friend's eyes lit up as she looked at Dale. "Maxine and I will be heading out too. Good job, Cliff." He shook Cliff's hand.

She hugged Maxine and whispered in her ear. "I'm happy for you and so glad you've come home to the island."

"Me too. Best friends are… well, the best." Maxine hugged her back before the couple walked away.

Cliff caught her arm. "Beverly, will you wait for me? I should only be a few minutes. Mother was right. We do need to talk."

Beverly stood outside the town hall, taking a moment to gather her thoughts as people milled around her. The evening breeze carried the scent of salt air, a familiar comfort that had always grounded her. She watched as Cliff shook hands with the last few council members, his smile genuine as they clapped him on the back.

When he finally turned and walked toward her, she was struck by how different he looked from the boy who had left Magnolia Key decades ago. His shoulders were broader, his stride more confident, but his eyes held the same intensity they always had when he looked at her.

"That was quite a surprise in there," she said as he approached.

"A good one, I hope." He stopped in front of her, hands in his pockets.

"A very good one. Why didn't you tell me about all these changes to your development plans? You never mentioned a word."

He glanced down at his shoes for a moment before meeting her eyes again. "I've been working on it since our conversation at dinner. I wanted to be sure I could pull it off before I said anything. The additional property only became available last week, and the redesigns had to be rushed through."

"But still, you could have mentioned it."

He shook his head slowly. "I didn't want to disappoint you if it fell through. These past few weeks, getting to know you again… it matters to me, Beverly. Your opinion of me matters."

The sincerity in his voice caught her off guard. She'd spent so many years holding onto her anger, and now it seemed to be slipping away like sand between her fingers.

"Well, I'm impressed," she admitted. "It's a beautiful design. The way you incorporated elements from the historical buildings, the environmental considerations—it's like you listened to everything everyone was concerned about."

"I did listen." He took a step closer. "Especially to you."

Warmth climbed through her. "Me?"

"When you talked about what makes Magnolia Key special, how the island has a certain magic about it, well, I realized I was thinking about the development all wrong. It shouldn't change the character of the place. It should enhance it."

Looking at him now, she saw a vulnerability behind his confidence. This wasn't just about a building project for him, it was about belonging.

"I'm proud of you, Cliff. But more importantly, you should be proud of yourself." She reached out and touched his arm lightly. "Your project is going to be a wonderful addition to the town."

"That means a lot coming from you. I know I've made mistakes—plenty of them. Running away from here was just one of many."

"We all make mistakes."

"True, but I'm hoping I can make up for some of mine." He took her hand in his, his thumb gently stroking her palm. "Starting with this project. I'd like your input as we finalize things—the landscaping, the historical exhibit, even some of the interior details."

She raised an eyebrow. "My input? I don't know anything about real estate development."

"No, but you know Magnolia Key better than anyone. You understand what makes this place special." He squeezed her hand. "We could work on it together. What do you say?"

The idea of collaborating with Cliff, of helping shape something that would become part of

Magnolia's future, appealed to her more than she would have thought possible a few weeks ago.

"I'd like that," she said finally.

The smile that spread across his face made her heart flutter the way it had started fluttering every time she saw him now. He took another step closer, close enough that she could smell his cologne mingling with the sea air.

"Beverly," he said softly, "I've been wanting to—"

Before he could finish, she rose up on her toes and pressed her lips to his. For a moment, he seemed surprised, but then his arms were around her, pulling her close as he returned the kiss with a tenderness that made her knees weak.

When they finally drew apart, she could hear her heart pounding in her ears. He looked down at her with wonder in his eyes, as if he couldn't quite believe what had just happened.

"I just wanted to surprise you tonight," she grinned at him.

"You can surprise me like that anytime you want."

Beverly thought about how much had changed since Cliff had returned to Magnolia Key. The hurricane, the rebuilding, and Eleanor's discovery of the letter he'd written all those years ago—all of it had somehow led them back to each other.

"This feels right, doesn't it?" She motioned between them.

"It does." He brushed a strand of hair from her face, his touch sending a shiver down her spine. "Like coming home after being away too long."

Beverly knew exactly what he meant. For years, she'd kept her heart carefully guarded, afraid to risk the pain of loss again. But standing here with Cliff, she felt something she hadn't experienced in a very long time—a sense of possibility and new beginnings.

"So," he said, taking her hand again, "partners?"

"Partners," she agreed, her fingers interlacing with his.

He smiled down at her, his eyes reflecting the same mix of hope and apprehension she felt. "Should we seal our partnership with another kiss?"

She laughed, feeling lighthearted and hopeful. "I think that would be appropriate."

As his lips met hers again, she thought about how life could surprise you when you least expected it. She'd spent decades believing that her chance at love had sailed away on that ferry with Cliff all those years ago. Now, somehow, they had found their way back to each other.

When they broke apart, he kept his arms around her, as if reluctant to let her go.

"What now?" She looked up into his eyes.

"Now," he said, "we build something beautiful together."

"Your development?"

"No… Us."

CHAPTER 28

Eleanor stood with Darlene at the small building at the edge of the beach, smoothing the jacket of her cream-colored suit. The fabric felt smooth and expensive beneath her fingers—a splurge she normally would have considered frivolous, but today was different. Today was special. Jonah was waiting for her at the gazebo.

She peered out the window at the white structure by the water, decorated with fresh flowers in shades of cream and pale blue. A small arbor overlooked the gentle waves of the gulf, the early evening sun painting everything in a golden glow.

"I still can't believe this moment is finally here," she said softly, more to herself than to Darlene. "After all these years."

"You look just lovely," Darlene said, adjusting the collar of Eleanor's suit.

She smiled, grateful for her old friend's presence. She and Darlene had shared so many of life's moments together—both joyful and painful. She was pleased they could share this one too.

"I'm glad we kept the actual ceremony small," she said, watching as a few guests made their way to the white chairs arranged on the gazebo. "Though I'm half afraid the whole town will be at the reception afterward at my house."

"Of course they will," Darlene laughed. "You're Eleanor Whitmore Griffin. Soon to be Eleanor Whitmore Burton. People respect you."

She caught Darlene's eyes in the reflection of the small mirror on the wall. "They rather fear me, you mean." She gave her friend a small smile.

"Perhaps a bit of both," Darlene conceded. "But they love you too. You've spent your whole life caring for this town, even if you did it with a stern look."

She turned away from the window, surveying the simple room where she'd chosen to prepare herself. No elaborate bridal suite or fuss—just a quiet moment to collect her thoughts before stepping into this new chapter.

"I spent too many years worried about what other people would think," she admitted. "Too many years letting that dictate my choices."

"It's never too late to change, is it?"

She nodded, thinking of Vera and the secret life

she'd lived with her prince. Her great-aunt had chosen love over duty, happiness over expectations. Eleanor was finally doing the same.

A knock sounded at the door, and her heart quickened. The door opened, and there stood Cliff, handsome in his dark suit, a small boutonniere in his lapel.

"Mother, you look beautiful."

"Why, thank you, Cliff."

"Are you ready?"

She felt a rush of emotion seeing her son standing there. Their relationship had transformed in recent months. The hurricane had done more than damage buildings—it had swept away years of misunderstanding between them, revealing the foundation of love that had always existed beneath.

"I've been ready for this day for what seems my whole life." Her voice sounded steady despite the flutter in her chest.

She crossed the room and took Cliff's offered arm, feeling the solid strength of him beside her. As they stepped outside, the early evening breeze carried the salty scent of the ocean, mingling with the fragrance of the flowers adorning the wedding site.

The small gathering of their closest friends turned to watch as she and Cliff began their walk toward the gazebo where Jonah waited.

She focused on Jonah standing beneath the

arbor, his face lighting up as he saw her. The years melted away, and suddenly, she was a young woman again, watching the handsome boy she'd first met, too shy to speak to him directly, too proper to acknowledge her feelings.

How different things might have been if she'd been braver then. If she hadn't let her parents' expectations and her own fear guide her choices. But there was no use dwelling on what might have been. Today was about what could be—what would be.

As they approached the gazebo, she squeezed Cliff's arm. "Thank you," she whispered, the words carrying more than just gratitude for escorting her down the aisle.

"I'm proud of you, Mother," her son replied softly. "For following your heart."

The simple words nearly brought tears to her eyes. For her son to speak of pride—the son she'd been so quick to criticize, so slow to understand—meant everything.

They reached the steps of the gazebo, and her gaze locked with Jonah's. His eyes, as blue as the gulf waters behind him, crinkled at the corners with his smile. He extended his hand to her as Cliff guided her up the steps.

"You look beautiful, Ellie," he said as she took her place beside him.

Her heart beat steadily as she faced Jonah, his

warm hands holding hers. The gulf breeze ruffled her carefully styled hair, but she no longer cared about perfection. The small gathering of their closest friends and family faded into the background as she focused on Jonah's face—the face she'd known for so many years, yet was seeing anew.

The minister's voice washed over them as he spoke of commitment and love in the autumn years of life. When it came time for their vows, she felt no nervousness, only a surprising calm.

"I, Eleanor, take you, Jonah, to be my husband." The words felt right on her lips, as though she'd been meant to say them all along. "To have and to hold, from this day forward, for better or worse, for richer or poorer, in sickness and in health, to love and to cherish, until death do us part."

Jonah's eyes never left hers as he repeated the same vows, his voice steady and sure. His hands trembled slightly in hers—not from uncertainty, she knew, but from the magnitude of the moment.

As Jonah slipped the simple gold band onto her finger, a profound sense of peace washed over her. All these years of yearning for this exact moment— a moment she'd long ago convinced herself would never come. A happiness she'd denied herself out of duty, out of pride, out of fear.

She gazed down at the ring on her finger, noting how right it looked there. All the worries about propriety and what people might think had vanished. She no longer cared about the whispers or judgments. At seventy-five, Eleanor had finally learned that life was too precious to waste on others' expectations.

"By the power vested in me, I now pronounce you husband and wife," the minister declared, his voice carrying across the gentle sound of waves breaking against the shore. He turned to the small gathering with a smile. "I present to you, Mr. and Mrs. Burton."

The small crowd applauded, and she caught sight of her son's face, filled with genuine happiness for her. She felt a surge of gratitude that they'd repaired their relationship in time for him to share this day with her.

The minister gave Jonah a conspiratorial smile and added, "Well, kiss your bride, Jonah. I hear she's been waiting a very long time."

A ripple of gentle laughter moved through their friends and family. She felt a blush rise to her cheeks.

And Jonah did kiss her. His lips met hers with a tenderness that spoke of both respect and passion. She found herself responding with more fervor than she'd intended, forgetting momentarily about their audience. When they finally parted, Jonah's eyes were twinkling with delight and surprise.

"Mrs. Burton," he whispered, just for her ears. "I've waited a lifetime to call you that."

After all her years of careful speech and measured words, she found herself speechless with joy.

Beverly watched as Eleanor and Jonah shared their first dance as husband and wife under the billowy white tent set up in Eleanor's backyard. Twinkling lights strung overhead cast a warm glow over the gathering of friends and family and townsfolk. The musicians played a slow melody that seemed to wrap around the couple like an embrace.

"They look so happy," Beverly said to Maxine, who stood beside her sipping champagne.

"They do," Maxine agreed. "Who would have thought Miss Eleanor would be dancing in her backyard at her own wedding reception?"

She smiled. "She's just Eleanor now, remember?"

"Old habits," Maxine said with a chuckle. "But seriously, have you ever seen her look so… content?"

She watched as Eleanor laughed at something Jonah whispered in her ear. There was a lightness to her now. "No, I haven't."

As the song ended, other couples moved to join the newlyweds on the makeshift dance floor. Dale extended his hand to Maxine, who handed Beverly her champagne glass before following him.

"Looks like it's just you and me," Cliff said, appearing beside her.

Her heart quickened at the sound of his voice. She turned to face him, taking in his navy suit and the way his eyes crinkled slightly at the corners when he smiled at her.

"Care to dance?" he asked, extending his hand.

She placed her hand in his and let him lead her to the dance floor. His arm circled her waist, and she rested her hand on his shoulder as they began to sway to the music.

"I'm not much of a dancer," he admitted, guiding her in a gentle circle.

"You're doing just fine," she assured him, enjoying the warmth of his palm against her lower back.

They moved in comfortable silence for a moment, the sounds of laughter and conversation creating a pleasant backdrop to the music. "You know," Cliff said, his voice low, meant only for her ears, "I've been thinking a lot about what you said about Magnolia Key. About preserving what makes it special."

She looked up at him, meeting his gaze.

"You made me see how important this place is," he continued. "Not just as a business opportunity, but as a home. *Our* home." His eyes held hers, filled with sincerity. "You made me remember why I love it here."

The breeze lifted a strand of hair across her face, and he gently tucked it behind her ear, his fingers lingering against her cheek.

"But it's not just Magnolia," he said softly. "It's you, Beverly. You're important to me. You always have been."

She felt like she had found the last missing piece to a jigsaw puzzle she'd spent most of her life working on. The doubts and hesitations that had lingered at the edges of her mind dissolved in the warmth of his gaze.

"Cliff." She stopped dancing, though his arms remained around her. Looking up into his eyes, she found the courage to say what she had known in her heart for some time. "I love you. I think maybe I always have, even when I tried not to."

His expression softened, and a smile spread across his face. He leaned down, his lips meeting hers in a kiss that felt like finally coming home.

"I've never stopped loving you, Beverly," he said, his voice thick with emotion. "Not for a single day since we were kids. Even when I left, even when I thought I'd never come back—it was always you. All I want is… you."

She closed her eyes, letting his words wash over her. The years of hurt and misunderstanding fell away, forgotten, leaving only this moment, leaving just the two of them.

The music played on as they began to sway

again, holding each other close under the canopy of lights, with the sea breeze and the sound of waves as their witnesses.

The moon looked down on Magnolia Key, shining its silvery light on the close-knit community. The small island town has a unique way of healing old wounds, mending friendships, and granting second chances. And for those in search of belonging… it shows them the way home.

Good night, Magnolia Key.

Dear Reader, I hope you enjoyed the Magnolia Key series. I'm so sad to leave these characters behind. I loved Miss Eleanor so much!

Up next is Starlight Shores. Pop over to my website to see the first book, Lighthouse Cottages.

In the meantime, did you know I have a standalone Christmas series? I add a book to it each year. This year I added Sweet River Holiday Homecoming. (Set in, you guessed it, Sweet River.)

As always, I'm so grateful for each one of you. You make my writing journey so meaningful.

May your days be filled with sunshine and warm breezes. Until next time… ~Kay

COMFORT CROSSING ~ THE SERIES

The Shop on Main - Book One

The Memory Box - Book Two

The Christmas Cottage - A Holiday Novella (Book 2.5)

The Letter - Book Three

The Christmas Scarf - A Holiday Novella (Book 3.5)

The Magnolia Cafe - Book Four

The Unexpected Wedding - Book Five

The Wedding in the Grove (crossover short story between series - Josephine and Paul from The Letter.)

LIGHTHOUSE POINT ~ THE SERIES

Wish Upon a Shell - Book One

Wedding on the Beach - Book Two

Love at the Lighthouse - Book Three

Cottage near the Point - Book Four

Return to the Island - Book Five

Bungalow by the Bay - Book Six

Christmas Comes to Lighthouse Point - Book Seven

CHARMING INN ~ Return to Lighthouse Point

One Simple Wish - Book One

Two of a Kind - Book Two

Three Little Things - Book Three

Four Short Weeks - Book Four

Five Years or So - Book Five

Six Hours Away - Book Six

Charming Christmas - Book Seven

SWEET RIVER ~ THE SERIES

A Dream to Believe in - Book One

A Memory to Cherish - Book Two

A Song to Remember - Book Three

A Time to Forgive - Book Four

A Summer of Secrets - Book Five

A Moment in the Moonlight - Book Six

MOONBEAM BAY ~ THE SERIES

The Parker Women - Book One

The Parker Cafe - Book Two

A Heather Parker Original - Book Three

The Parker Family Secret - Book Four

Grace Parker's Peach Pie - Book Five

The Perks of Being a Parker - Book Six

BLUE HERON COTTAGES ~ THE SERIES

Memories of the Beach - Book One

Walks along the Shore - Book Two

Bookshop near the Coast - Book Three

Restaurant on the Wharf - Book Four

Lilacs by the Sea - Book Five

Flower Shop on Magnolia - Book Six

Christmas by the Bay - Book Seven

Sea Glass from the Past - Book Eight

MAGNOLIA KEY ~ THE SERIES

Saltwater Sunrise - Book One

Encore Echoes - Book Two

Coastal Candlelight - Book Three

Tidal Treasures - Book Four

Bayside Beginnings - Book Five

Seaside Sunshine - Book Six

Boardwalk Breezes - Book Seven

CHRISTMAS SEASHELLS AND SNOWFLAKES

Seaside Christmas Wishes

WIND CHIME BEACH ~ A stand-alone novel

INDIGO BAY ~

Sweet Days by the Bay - Kay's complete collection of stories in the Indigo Bay series

ABOUT THE AUTHOR

Kay Correll is a USA Today bestselling author of sweet, heartwarming stories that are a cross between women's fiction and contemporary romance. She is known for her charming small towns, quirky townsfolk, and the enduring strong friendships between the women in her books.

Kay splits her time between the southwest coast of Florida and the Midwest of the U.S. and can often be found out and about with her camera, taking a myriad of photographs, often incorporating them into her book covers. When not lost in her writing or photography, she can be found spending time with her ever-supportive husband, knitting, or playing with her puppies - a cavalier who is too cute for his own good and a naughty but adorable Australian shepherd. Their five boys are all grown now and while she misses the rowdy boy-noise chaos, she is thoroughly enjoying her empty nest years.

Learn more about Kay and her books at kaycorrell.com

While you're there, sign up for her newsletter to hear about new releases, sales, and giveaways.

WHERE TO FIND ME:
My shop: shop.kaycorrell.com
My author website: kaycorrell.com
authorcontact@kaycorrell.com

Join my Facebook Reader Group. We have lots of fun and you'll hear about sales and new releases first!
www.facebook.com/groups/KayCorrell/

I love to hear from my readers. Feel free to contact me at authorcontact@kaycorrell.com

facebook.com/KayCorrellAuthor

instagram.com/kaycorrell

pinterest.com/kaycorrellauthor

amazon.com/author/kaycorrell

bookbub.com/authors/kay-correll